Thanks once again again to Madison Kopp for keeping my covers from being disasters. If you're as obsessed with her as I am, you can check out the other things she's doing at @riddlemethisreads on Tiktok!

Content Warnings on Page 215

Nonymous

To everyone except my high school debate team.

Rory: 8 Days Before Projected Impact

One of these days, I am going to kill Finn Williams.

She'll probably even smile while I do it.

I watch them talk to Mr. Barber. Everything about Finn—her posture, her gestures, her very expressions—is big and obvious. She always has been. Finn isn't looking any more forward to being partnered up again than I am, but if they're going to insist on not admitting that, the least they can do is make it less obvious that they're more disgusted by me than the prospect of not competing at all. I have no issue with dishonesty. It's when you're as shit at hiding it as Finn is that I begin to get offended. Still, as she turns around to pretend to notice my presence in the room, she's smiling.

"Hey!" They jog over. "Enzo's parents are too worried about him leaving town next week, so Mr. Barber asked me to sub in. Looks like we'll just have to kick ass together again."

I don't bother hiding my sigh because unlike Finn, I'm not afraid of acknowledging that we both hate being paired up like this. We've been Rory and Finn since the first tournament I was out for—or Finn and Rory if you ask anyone but me, but I try to avoid getting other people's opinions on my life whenever possible. Finn's little group of sycophants used to think that it was somehow noble of her to be seen around me.

"Aww, Finn's teaming up with Rory to make sure she can still compete even if she is a bitch."

"Finn's such a good debater that he doesn't think pairing up with Rory'll hurt his score, even if she decides to get all pissy again every time the judges or opposing team call her 'miss' or 'she'."

"Finn doesn't even get mad when Rory performs the totally unreasonable act of asking judges to get their fucking pronouns right."

Judges are supposed to be impartial, but they never are. Not really. When your very identity is a site of debate, it's hard for that not to influence people who base their entire lives around arguing. Unless you're Finn fucking Williams who's willing to let anyone misgender her for a quick win.

Some of us have more self-respect than that.

Finn was never actually volunteering to be my partner just because they were kind or noble or even because she recognized that I was an excellent debater. They were just a closeted nonbinary kid looking for someone to live through vicariously. And now she's an out nonbinary kid still stuck with me because everyone just assumes that we'll get along simply because we're both queer.

"I can talk to Enzo," I tell them. "I'm sure—"

"His parents threatened to pull him out of school if we try to bring him."

"I'll call his parents then."

"Rory." She grabs my arm. You don't spend all of high school sharing buses and hotel rooms with someone without knowing when they're about to storm out of a room to do exactly whatever ill-advised thing they've just decided to do. "He's not coming. You can give me his notes and even if they suck, I've been coaching all of the practices. I probably have more points than you guys do. We'll be fine."

I hate knowing that she's right. No matter how much I can't stand Finn Williams and their constant refusal to ever shake the boat even an inch, they're an objectively excellent debater. We're objectively excellent debaters together. I've been molding Enzo to be the perfect partner since he showed a smidge of potential at the beginning of the year and even he's not up to Finn's caliber yet. I've come to terms with that though. I'd take a slightly subpar partner over having to share my last victory of the year with Finn any day.

"I was already going to come help judge," she continues. "It seriously won't be a big change."

"What if we qualify for provincials?"

Finn frowns at me. We have never once qualified for provincials. "Then we'll see if they'll let someone else sub in for me."

It makes sense, in theory. Finn's made it perfectly clear that her priorities won't align properly come provincials season but by the time that rolls around, Enzo's parents will have to admit that they're just being paranoid. I'll probably even be able to bring him, just like I'd originally planned. But Finn would always get to know that she'd helped us get there.

"You know," they say slowly, bouncing from heel to toe. They've done that since we were kids. If I had to pick one word to describe Finn physically, it wouldn't be "freakishly tall" or "brunette" or "that person with the annoyingly bright brown eyes", it would be bouncy. "You could just drop out. They're offering refunds to anyone who—"

"We're doing the fucking tournament," I stop her.

"Okay." They stand there bouncing awkwardly for another second before jerking a thumb back towards the whiteboard. "I'd better umm... club to run and all that."

I roll my eyes as they make their escape. I've never told her that it's a sore spot—I'll never tell her that it's a sore spot at all, she'd probably secretly gloat about it the moment she was home alone and capable of gloating without ruining her perfect little image—but I will never not resent that Finn was chosen to run the team for our final year of high school while I'd never even made exec. On paper, it makes no sense. Finn and I are equally strong debaters. Our styles and approaches couldn't be more removed from each other, but if I get a better score one tournament you can always expect to see Finn's name somewhere within five spots of mine and vice versa. We've both been consistently outperforming everyone else on the team since tenth grade so one of us being president was a given. The other not being made vice president was clearly personal, but I couldn't even make a case against it.

Finn's been out as agender since tenth grade—a fact that the faculty and the rest of the club conveniently seem to only remember when spouting off inclusivity BS—so of course there's no possible was that the team she runs could be refusing to award someone else because of a gender bias. If given the choice to pick between the lesser of two gender-nonconforming evils, everyone is always going to pick Finn. Not because they're better than me, they just make it a lot more convenient for cis people to use her for brownie points.

Again, self-respect.

Finn and the rest of the execs start talking, but I tune it all out to go through my notes. I'm not arrogant, I'm just practical. With the possible exception of Finn, I could outperform any of them any day and I'm sure I'll get to hear way too many of her 'tips' on the way to the tournament next week. It makes the most sense to spend the beginning of the meeting going over my notes and plotting ways to murder Enzo. He hasn't arrived yet. Maybe he's trying to avoid coming altogether. If I were him, I would. But then just as we're about to pair up, he walks through the door. Mr. Barber must not have told him that he was going to tell me that Enzo had bailed, because the little traitor makes the mistake of smiling at me for a moment before realizing that I'm definitely not smiling back and sheepishly walking over.

"Sorry," he whispers.

I don't respond, deciding that it's the perfect opportunity to give my full attention to the exec team for the first time this year. Once we split up to go find our rooms though, he's unavoidable.

"Rory!" Enzo jogs after me.

I'd taken off the moment we'd gotten our room numbers, but it's hard to avoid someone when you're headed towards the same place. I'm not a fan of fake apologies, but we're going to have to talk about it at some point. I reluctantly slow down and let him catch up.

"I'm sorry," he says again. "My parents really aren't comfortable with me going."

"This was my last chance, Enzo," I remind him.

"I know." But he doesn't. Enzo's only in eleventh grade. He'll still have a shot at making it to provincials next year. Not with me there to help him qualify which will definitely be a massive setback, but it would still be possible, at least.

"There's still time," I inform him. "Your name's probably still down. If we talk to your parents together, maybe we could–"

He scratches his leg. It's his tell.

"You don't want to come," I realize.

He sighs. "People are saying–"

"People are fucking nutjobs!"

He stares at his shoes. I sigh and continue on towards our assigned room. Count on the cosmos to even be conspiring against me.

Last week, NASA made the mistake of leaking to the public that some giant, potentially world-ending asteroid was currently on route towards our side of the globe. It only took them a day to announce that they'd actually successfully rerouted it weeks ago, but the most paranoid of conspiracy nuts are still convinced that it's heading our way. The most paranoid of conspiracy nuts and, apparently, the eleventh grader I picked out for myself at the beginning of the year because I thought that he'd seemed like the most level-headed of our recruits. The debunked impact wasn't even projected to happen until the Tuesday after the tournament, so he and his parents are being extra paranoid.

So maybe Enzo wouldn't have been the best of partners after all. Whatever. Anyone would be better than Finn fucking Williams.

Rory: 14 Years Before Impact

The first day I met Finn, I figured out her secret.

We were eternally paired together in grade school. That was just what happened when your last names were too similar. So, on the second day of kindergarten, we were seated together at the Lego station.

Finn was building a tower big enough to be a safety hazard and the moment I reached out and dared to take a single block for me own pathetic little house, they exploded. They were smart though, even at four. A tiny curly haired menace.

They screamed, pushing their own tower into me. It shattered on impact and they screamed louder.

Our teacher came running over, consoled a sobbing Finn, and sent me to go sit in the cubby hall to 'think about how my actions affected others'.

Fine smiled back at me as the teacher guided them away.

I've never forgotten that. That no matter how nice or innocent Finn pretends to be, she's the kind of person who would destroy themself just for the opportunity to drag someone else down with her.

Rory: 7 Days Before Projected Impact

"You could just not go, Rore."

Alice—my best friend turned girlfriend turned ex turned best friend again—doesn't understand the importance of this final debate tournament. She never has.

"I'm obviously still going."

She sighs a bit, sitting down at our regular lunch table. "Then that's your choice. You don't get to spend the rest of the week complaining about Finn again just because you're too stubborn to miss a tournament."

I busy myself with pulling out my lunch bag because if I don't, I know we'll get into another argument. That's been happening a lot more recently, since we broke up last summer. Maybe it's because she's secretly still bitter that I broke up with her. Maybe it's because I'm secretly still bitter that I'm still a bit in love with her. It's hard to tell.

"They could have paired me up with someone else," I point out.

Alice raises an eyebrow. Hers are thick and neat and always drawn in to uniform perfect. It's part of the reason I like her. Even Alice's eyebrows are consistent. "Who?"

I pretend to look for something in my lunch bag.

She sighs. "He's rescuing you, Rory. The least you can do is—"

"She's not rescuing anyone. They've probably been waiting to find a way to weasel their way into this since I told them I was pairing up with someone else."

Alice frowns at me.

"What?"

"Not everyone's as obsessed with this stuff as you are."

Finn is though. It's one of her best and only redeeming qualities. Alice got paired up with her on a bio project last year though and she's gone dark side ever since. Sometimes that feels more traitorous than our breakup was.

"All I'm saying," she continues "is that you could at least try to be nice. If—"

"Can we stop talking about Finn?" I snap.

Alice stares at me. Her hand lands on the table—centimeters away from mine—but then she pulls it back. "Okay."

We lapse into silence.

That's another reason I hate Finn Williams, though it's less exciting because unlike most of their annoying qualities, this one isn't actually her fault.

Ever since she thought I was a girl and I thought he was a boy, people have just assumed that we'd end up together. It was stupid stuff, in elementary school. Before Finn learned how to be polite and friendly and boring, she was an absolute menace. All pulled pigtails and stolen toys and fart noises and mean jokes. Since I used to be the one with the stronger moral compass, I'd fight back. By second grade, pretty much all of their elementary school vitriol was targeted at me.

When a kid people think is a girl and a kid people think is a boy are constantly harassing each other, straight adults call them soulmates because—according to Facebook memes and sitcoms—straight marriages are built upon foundations of hatred and mutually assured destruction. When you reach high school and continue to hate each other, your incredibly cool girlfriend who wasn't even there for all of the creepy elementary school marriage comments starts saying things like, "can't you stay with someone else this tournament?" or, "I'm not comfortable with how often you have Finn over" or even just, "you talk about them a lot, huh?" as if she didn't used to be incredibly aware that you felt nothing but annoyance for said arch nemesis.

Finn didn't break us up, but she could have. They got close a few times last year. And if I'm going to fix Alice so we can get back together again, her suddenly trying to push me to be nicer to the person she used to be jealous of isn't a good sign.

I reach across our booth when the silence becomes too thick. I link our pinkies together.

"Sorry," I say. "It's just..."

"Stressful times," she finishes for me. Alice is good at that, figuring out the words that don't make it past my brain. "I get it. My parents are freaking out at each other even more than usual with all this space BS."

"And it's my last tournament," I remind her. I know potential apocalypses outrank things like that, but I still find myself a bit annoyed that that wasn't what she thought of first. Alice doesn't believe in all the panic on the news anyway and if it were one of her piano competitions coming up, I would have remembered to mention it. Especially if we'd literally just been talking about it.

"Right," she smiles. "I'm sure you'll crush it. Finn or no Finn."

"Love you," I say. Platonically, for now. Platonically, like we used to.

"I know," she says. "We're fine."

"Will we be finer if I buy you apology ice cream?"

Alice grins. "I think that might help."

Rory: 5 Days Before Projected Impact

Every other team has probably been working together for months, so I force Finn to get together with me every night leading up to the tournament to practice. We always meet at my place. We've spent countless afternoons together, but I still don't even know their address. Finn says it's because her house is too busy to focus in, but I'm pretty sure she's just a lot more aware of our unofficial rivalry than she likes to pretend she is and knows how risky it would be to let me know where she lives.

I wouldn't do anything, obviously, but it's nice to know that they find me intimidating.

Finn and I have different preparation methods so when we work together, it always takes twice as long. They're always focused on our own points. She comes up with the strongest arguments for and against each motion and spends all of her time developing that. Despite how many times I've tried to make her do otherwise, they can't seem to grasp the importance of focusing on your opposition.

You could have the best arguments in the world, but they won't mean anything if you can't guess what your opponent is going to say and anticipate how you're going to pull their points apart. So, every other practice, I make us prepare my way. We take turns running potential arguments that neither of us have any intention of actually using just so the other person can strengthen their counterpoints. Finn thinks it's a waste of time, but I know better. The most effective way to debate is to imagine what your opposition would say. That's a lot easier to do with a teammate than alone in my bedroom, talking to the air.

We get through a semi-productive half hour of countering each other's arguments that Thursday which is why it makes absolutely no sense when Finn flops down onto my couch and sighs.

"I've been talking to my parents," she says.

I freeze. I know what that did to my last partner. "No."

"They're worried about me going. They want me home in case—"

"You had to wait until the last fucking second to say something?"

They wince, but I know Finn Williams. Perhaps better than anyone.

"You did this on purpose."

She sighs. "Rory, I didn't—"

"No," I point a finger at them. "You couldn't stand the thought of me doing this without you, could you? You were never actually planning on—"

"Rory," they say again. "I'm not you."

"What the fuck does that mean!"

Finn just sighs again. "Look, I'm sorry, okay? It's only last minute because I've been fighting myself about it. This has nothing to do with you. I've never been as... I don't know. Weirdly antagonistic as you are?"

She has been and she knows it. She has always been and she knows it.

"You can still go and judge, if you want," they continue. "I emailed Mr. Barber and he said—"

"When?"

They wince. They know that I've caught them. "This morning, but—"

"You've known you were bailing this whole time!" Pacing is supposed to help you blow off steam but in my case, it's always just made me more antsy. I do it anyway. It's a bad habit. "You let me research and practice knowing—"

"You're not exactly the easiest person to reason with!"

I force my bouncing legs to bend and sit in my father's armchair to watch her. I am not about to miss my last tournament. Not now when I finally feel like I might actually have a shot at placing high enough to qualify for provincials.

"Maybe someone else'll bail too. You can pair up with—"

"I won't win with someone else!"

Finn stares at me, failing miserably to hide the tension in their cheeks as they fight off a grin. I've never understood why everyone else seems to think that she's a good actor.

"That wasn't a compliment," I grumble. "It's just a fact. You're good at debate. Statistically."

She rolls her eyes. "I'm not changing my mind just because you're being semi-nice."

"I'm not being semi-nice. I told you, it's just a fact. Nothing personal."

We're both quiet. I squeeze my fingers between my knees. "If I really was semi-nice, would you—"

"No."

I nod. It wasn't a real offer anyway. Sometimes I think that Finn and I were created to drive each other insane.

"I'm sorry," she says.

"It's fine," I lie. I'm already realizing that it will be. "Hope you guys enjoy Asia."

"I... what?"

I shrug. "You must be heading over there, right? With your secret private plane because everything else is booked solid until after the impact's supposed to happen?"

"You can't manipulate me into going, Rory," they start to get up.

"I'm not." I stand too. If my body's between her and the exit now, that's just a coincidence. "I'm just being logical. If a magical evil space rock is hurtling towards us, you'd be just as fucked two hours from here are you would be if you stayed in town."

"I'd be with my family."

"You can videocall them," I shrug. "I'll carry a power bank and everything. You get first dibs of it if an apocalypse starts mid-motion."

Brown eyes scan my basement as if someone will appear from behind a couch to rescue her. Finn's nothing if not a people pleaser. "Rory, I can't..."

They trail off. Finn's aways full of words so if she's not, it means I've already won.

"Please," I try. It's a new word for Finn and I, but it comes out more easily than anything I've ever said. There's no shame in a little light groveling if it helps you get what you want. "Then if we qualify Enzo can switch back in and you can go do pre-show week–"

"Tech week," she corrects.

"Yeah, whatever. And then you never have to talk to me ever again, alright? Just this one last thing. You owe me this one last thing."

I'm awful with change and Finn knows it. It's not fair of them to do this so close to a tournament. They deserve a little light manipulating.

She taps her fingers against her jeans. Tilts her head up towards the ceiling just that little bit they always do when they're thinking. "I'll talk to my parents, okay? No promises though."

I've already won. Finn Williams would commit murder before she'd ever willingly let someone down.

Rory: 10 Years Before Impact

One of the most annoying things about declaring a rivalry with Finn Williams was how good they were at everything. Sometimes, it was hard to keep up.

If there was a reading challenge, I'd always have to be exactly one book ahead. A fundraising event and I'd bother all the adults in my life until I was ahead by a dollar.

I slipped up one month, in second grade. Whoever read the most books each month got to choose the movie we'd watch and I'd accidentally let us tie.

The teacher pulled us aside, showed us our options, and asked us to agree. I think she already knew that we'd never agree. Even if we both did have the same favourite, we'd never admit to it because we were Rory and Finn.

So, she said "let's flip a coin."

Finn called out tails right away, I got stuck with heads, and she won. Our teacher decided that it was a genius conflict resolution strategy and kept using it and at some point it—and our answers—stuck.

Rory: 4 Days Before Projected Impact

To get to the tournament, we have to take two buses, a train, and then a third bus. It's excessive and a massive waste of time, but you need to make sacrifices when you're from a town without a thriving local debate community.

Debate in general's been suffering recently. Each area used to hold one regional qualifier but last year, they started letting anyone who placed first in any bigger external tournaments compete as well. That means that I should have qualified already. That means that I'm not going to accept that I didn't. I'd drag us all over the province if it upped our chances, but I've never managed to get the rest of the team to agree to that. A lot of them are only debate kids because it looks good on university applications. I'm a debate kid because I need to be. Seven-minute speeches about random topics that I'm usually more than half pretending to care about are the only times I truly feel like me.

Case in point, Finn's the only exec going to this tournament. Everyone else checked out pretty much right when university essays were due, and she only ended up coming because I bullied her into it. We squirrel away on the back of buses and a way too full GO Train car with a group of still eager ninth and tenth grader's that Finn's somehow now responsible for as the de facto adult. I should probably count as one too since we're the same age, but if Mr. Barber couldn't be bothered to join us himself or to acknowledge that I should have been made an exec, I don't feel like jumping through hoops to help him.

So, I'm studying. Finn, notably, is not. In grade nine I used to be able to pressure them into using the trip to tournaments to fit in some extra prep time, but in tenth they vetoed that in favour of goofing off with their friends. Now that none of her friends are present she at least sits with me, but nods off to whatever's playing through her sticker-covered headphones instead of paying attention to the sheets I've given up on trying to get them to read.

"What are you doing?" Some ninth grader I haven't bothered to learn the name of leans over Finn to ask me.

"Prepping."

"Wanna swap notes? We can—"

Finn—who, of course, has been secretly eavesdropping the whole time—opens one eye. "They're not studying anything relevant. Rory always prints off an absurd amount of random news stories to memorize on the way over because they think they'll somehow be able to guess what the impromptu rounds will be about."

I kick her foot. "I might."

"They won't. They never have."

"Impromptu rounds are normally more general though, right?" The random debater suddenly looks nervous. I realize that this is probably their first tournament. I know that that means that we should be reassuring them so they don't freeze up their first round, but I also know that I can just leave that to Finn. I don't have time for people who aren't invested enough to go to tournaments until the end of the year.

"They are," Finn, predictably, comforts them. "Especially this one. It's normally super liberal, at least one motion will probably just be gender or identity politics."

"Oh," the kid says. They turn their attention back to me. "You must be excited for that."

I flinch. Finn catches it and puts a hand on my knee to try and stop me from tackling a random grade nine, but I shake their hand off. "What's that supposed to mean?"

The kid frowns, staring at the rainbow pins on my bag. "I just meant... you're gay, right?"

"Pan," I correct. "And nonbinary. That doesn't mean I love arguing about my own identity."

"Oh," she blushes. "Right."

"Just because I'm queer doesn't mean everyone should just expect me to be an expert on queer issues," I point out. I am, but just because I like to be an expert on everything. "Identity motions shouldn't even be allowed, they're too personal. Not everyone gets to pretend to have equal stake in either side."

"Sorry," she squeaks. "I just... Finn seems to like those motions, so I thought—"

"Not all queer people are the same. Plus Finn's like, barely queer. That doesn't count."

She freezes beside me. You'd think I'd be better at choosing my words for someone obsessed with using them.

"Wait," I realize. "I didn't—"

When Finn stands up, they're smiling. They're always smiling. "Come on," they tell the ninth grader. "Let's go see how ready everyone else is feeling."

"Finn," I grab their arm. "I obviously wasn't—"

They shake me off, so annoyingly positive that Random Grade Nine probably doesn't even realize that I've fucked up. "I'm just gonna go give the rest of the team a peptalk."

But she never returns to her seat.

"Finn," I speedwalk to catch up with her after she's finished roll call at our final bus stop.

"Let's go everyone!" They announce, turning away from me to follow the directions on their phone. I sigh, jogging to keep up with their obnoxiously long strides. Having a partner pissed at you right before the most important tournament of your life isn't exactly ideal.

She's not evil enough to make me actually run to keep up with her though. Not quite.

"We're not arguing in front of the team," she hisses once I fall into pace beside her.

I bite my tongue. If I'm the one apologizing, I know I'll have to do it on their terms. "Okay. Fine."

We keep walking in silence. And then we arrive at our destination and we're anything but.

"What the fuck."

"It's fine," Finn smiles as the rest of the team echoes similar sentiments. They adjust their backpack strap and stand a bit taller. "It's different. Modern."

It's a lot of things, but it's definitely not a hotel. We stand in front of a rickety farmhouse right out of some horribly outdated western. It stands tall and looming in the middle of a field, protected only by a breaking fence seemingly patched time and time again with more nailed on pieces of wood. I'm pretty sure there are shingles on the lawn.

"This can't be–"

"This is it!" Finn declares, as if not letting anyone voice their dismay will keep it from existing.

It was never a question of whether or not we were at the right house. There aren't any other buildings within eyesight. I'm not responsible for the rest of the team, not technically, but it'd still feel wrong letting a bunch of young teens walk into a probable murder house. I lean towards Finn.

"Maybe we should–" I don't know what I'm planning on suggesting. Wander back into town to try and find an actual hotel. Take over the gym of the building hosting the tournament. A little light breaking and entering. It's too late for any of that anyway.

An old lady's making her way towards us, apron partly untied and three quarters of her hair still in curlers. She looks like someone who got halfway into their 'Universal Grandma Cosplay' then got too distracted to ever finish.

"Hello!" She waves. Her nails are red. That, at least, is completed to perfection. "Is one of you Finneas Williams?"

Finn waves back. My heart sinks directly down to my ass.

There's no way they'd ever let an old lady down. We're fucked.

Rory: 4 Days Before Projected Impact

The woman running the bed and breakfast/hostel/under the table AirBNB—"call me Madge", apparently—leads us into a house that's slightly less decrepit than its exterior. The walls are covered in tiny blue birds and the marble fireplace mantal is cracked in a few places but other than that, most of the house at least seems to have been built in this century.

Finn politely excuses herself to go take a hushed phone call with Mr. Barber in the corner, leaving me as the only remaining semi-adult.

"Your house is unique," I tell Madge. "Antique."

"Thank you," she says, unconcerned with whether or not it was supposed to be a compliment. I awkwardly perch on the arm of a plastic covered chair because sitting in discomfort feels oddly better than standing in it. The six kids we've hauled here with us slowly follow suit.

We watch Madge. She watches us. Somewhere, a clock ticks. I never thought I'd miss Finn's penchant for small talk.

"Alright," she eventually grins her way back over. "We're good to go! Just had to handle a few things back at the school."

When Madge smiles at them, it's genuine. Everyone's like that with Finn. It's insufferable.

"Thank you so much for opening your home to us."

"Of course, dear," she says. "I..." her eyes scan our group, forehead growing more and more wrinkled. She pushes up her glasses. "Oh my, there are eight of you?"

"Is that... will that be a problem?" For once, Finn looks at least a little worried.

Madge's smile grows. "One moment. Let me go talk to my husband."

There's no more space on any of the couches, so Finn crouches down in front of us. "All the hotels nearby are super booked up," she whispers. "People are freaking out about the asteroid and wanted to be near family, I guess." She doesn't look at me. She's Finn Williams, so it's probably not even an intentional dig to try and make me feel guilty for dragging her along. It doesn't work, but my jaw twitches regardless. "Barber found this place in some old B&B directory so we're gonna crash here for the weekend and pretend it's totally normal, okay?"

None of us challenge them.

"Finneas, dear," Madge pokes her head back into the room. "Would you mind coming here for a moment?"

The grade nine from the bus grabs their arm. "Don't go alone," she whispers.

Finn rolls their eyes. "I'll be fine. She's just a sweet old woman."

The sweet old woman shuts the door behind her though, so I tighten my fist around the pencil in my pocket. Just in case.

"Okay!" Finn claps once as they jog back over to us. She does that a lot, the clapping. And the bouncing and humming and smiling and gesturing.

A list of more accurate words to describe Finn Williams than 'nice': bouncy, loud.

"Seems we had a bit of a mix up. With a lot of people dropping and rejoining, we under booked."

I scoff a little at that since I know the 'lot of people' in question is the very person talking. Finn's moved to stand right next to me though, so no one notices. It's hard to notice anyone around her.

"Madge here," she nods at Madge and I swear the old woman blushes, "talked to her husband on our behalf and they've offered to let two of us stay in the old storm bunker—"

"Anti-alien chamber!" Comes a gravelly voice from the kitchen.

Finn just keeps nodding. "Right. Anyway, as long as we swear we'll be gone by Tuesday they said two of us could use it instead! They literally just restocked it and changed the sheets and stuff so it'll be perfect."

As little as I want to stay in some random strangers' freaky paranoia bunker, I know that Finn would hate it more. I don't need a shaken debate partner tomorrow morning.

I point to the ninth grader from the bus. "You and your roommate can take the bunker."

She just blinks at me.

Finn laughs. "Rory's kidding. We want you guys close to each other so you can practice if you want to. We'll take it."

I frown. "Finn."

"Rory." They jab a finger into my back where no one else can see it. Finn is exceptionally pointy. "Anyways," for everyone else, she's all smiles. "Madge was just telling me about this awesome diner a few roads over if anyone wanted to join. I'll pay."

That automatically means that everyone's going to join.

They turn to me. "Bunker's on the other end of the field. We're free to use the living room but if you wanted to set up there, I'm sure Madge or her husband can show you how to get to it."

It's not a not-so-subtle way of excluding me from dinner. Finn knows that I'm not going because I never do anymore. I come to tournaments equipped with a bag of snacks and duotangs of research. Still, I choose to believe that it's an intentional insult.

"I'm sure someone'll swap rooms with us if–"

"Rory," they repeat.

I nod once. I don't need an even more pissed off partner and at least now she won't be able to blame me for not try.

A list of more accurate words to describe Finn Williams than 'nice': bouncy, loud, claustrophobic.

"Okay." I try to mimic her energetic grin as I turn to Madge. I doubt it works. "Let's check out this alien room."

Rory: 5 Years Before Impact

In seventh grade, for the first time, we got to choose our assigned reading books. It was only from a list of five, but that still sounded significant. I chose *Fahrenheit 451* because it was by far the most famous and therefore intellectual sounding book on the list and I wanted everyone else to know how smart I was.

The downstairs grade seven class had the same selection of books to choose from and our school wasn't fancy enough to spring for enough copies of those five books for each class, so every day our teacher would ask for a pair of volunteers to retrieve the book cart using the school's one and only elevator. Finn was entering her public image redemption arc that year, so they always volunteered. I always did too because I'd be damned if I was going to let Finn Williams seem like a better student than me.

Seventh grade was the avoidance period of our rivalry. When adults assuming that kids they that thought were boys and kids that they thought were girls hating each other meant that they were secretly in love started to feel more embarrassing than annoying because we were becoming old enough for our own real secret crushes. Mine was on Tim Byrd, an eighth grader who'd been in my split class the year before who I'd barely ever talked to. Finn's was, presumably, on someone, because they also started avoiding me whenever they could.

We picked up the cart without talking to each other like we usually did. Finn walked ahead to press the elevator button because despite it only having two floors to cover, it always took forever to arrive. I pushed the books. We were awkward and silent around each other, but I'd known Finn long enough that falling into routines always happened silently seamlessly.

We boarded the elevator like we usually did. Finn pressed the button. Then, everything shook. At the time, it felt so drastic that I swore the world went blurry, but not a single book fell off the cart so it couldn't have been that serious. Then the shaking stopped and the doors stayed closed and we were both still silent.

She whispered my old name because I hadn't chosen my real one yet.

I thought she was asking what was going on, so I said, "we're stuck. There's probably an emergency phone or button or something."

I checked and sure enough, there was a phone button. I pressed it and waited.

They whispered the wrong name again.

"It's probably because the school's old, you know?" I continued. "I doubt they do regular maintenance checks on an elevator that basically no one uses."

No voice came through the speaker, so I hit the button again. "I'm not sure if they connect this thing to the office or first responders, but either way it shouldn't take this long for—"

"Shut up!"

I blinked. Turned around. Finn was sitting between the wall and book cart, knees pulled to their chest, and breath far too loud loud. I wasn't sure how I hadn't noticed it before because once I clicked into the sound, it was the only thing I could hear.

"You're having a panic attack." I informed her.

Finally, a voice crackled through the speakers. I let them know that we were stuck, waited for confirmation that they'd called the fire department to come help, and sat back down across from a still panicking Finn.

"You're having a panic attack," I repeated. "Has that happened before?"

They shook their head.

"Crap. Do you know what to do?"

She shook her head again.

"They've already sent people, you know," I informed her. "There's seriously nothing to worry about."

"I need out now," she whispered. Their voice was fast and high and breathy.

"Well, that's not happening. But it will, you know. When they come." I paused. "Maybe you're claustrophobic. Are you claustrophobic?"

They were crying and panting so it took a moment before they said, "maybe?"

That didn't give me any helpful information. I didn't know how to deal with claustrophobia or non-claustrophobia themed panic attacks.

"Well, the elevator's still the same size as it's always been so nothing scary there."

That didn't calm her down.

"And you've kind of made yourself a tiny little corner there with the cart? Maybe move?"

She didn't.

I sighed, getting up to push the cart myself. They reached out to keep it in place, so I sat back down.

"They're coming," I said again. "Soon. Maybe umm... read a book or something?"

They pushed away tears with the back of their hand. "you're bad at this."

I rolled my eyes. "Not my fault you decided to freak out over a freaking elevator."

I found the least bent copy of *Fahrenheit 451,* leaned against the opposite wall, and waited for help to arrive.

She must have calmed down slightly at some point, because Finn eventually interrupted me with "tell anyone I freaked out and I'll tell them that you just sat there and did nothing."

I glanced up to confirm that their face was slightly less red. "Yeah, whatever."

I returned my focus to my book, but not before catching them mutter "bitch".

"crybaby."

I could read her even in silence by that point, so when she pulled back to kick me, I was ready for it. I hit the side of the cart to block her and smiled to myself as I heard their foot connect with metal.

Rory: 4 Days Before Projected Impact

"So," I decide to make an attempt at small talk as Madge escorts me through a field that's seemingly growing nothing more than mud and tall grass.

She'd pulled on long rubber boots before leading me out the backdoor and asked if I wanted to change my own shoes. As if I'd realized a debate tournament would require rainboots. Tournaments don't technically have a dress code beyond "don't wear anything offensive", but business-casual to full out business is always implied. I'm glad I have my dress shoes safely stowed away in my bag. I always aim for full business.

"Was the bunker here before you guys moved in or..."

"It's Roy's ancestral home," she says.

She seems almost offended that I would imply otherwise so I just say, "oh. Right."

"It used to be an old storm shelter, but his brothers and father fixed it up just before Y2K. It's all very high tech."

"Right," I repeat.

"I suppose it'll finally come in handy again. What, with the asteroid and what not."

"Right."

So much for small talk.

Everything about the emergency bunker screams "you're about to be murdered." The door's located so far away from the farmhouse that it's little more than a spec in the distance. It's some kind of heavy metal that Madge needs to ask me to open. Her unseen husband had better be strong or they'll end up stuck down there if they're really planning on hiding on Tuesday. I pull up on the metal ring serving as a handle and Madge says, "don't worry dear, it locks from the inside."

It's the kind of thing that you don't worry about until someone tells you to. I don't ask about the why either. A lock wouldn't be all that helpful if the rest of the world was fried on impact, but maybe they fall on the 'the asteroid's an alien space ship' end of the conspiracy spectrum and I really don't feel like getting into that.

We descend down a dark ladder towards who knows what. Madge keeps assuring me she'll turn on the light at the bottom, but it doesn't lessen the alarm bells going off as I follow a stranger deep into the earth. I could overpower her. Probably.

All at once, my feet are back on solid ground. It makes me stumble. Madge must find the switch, because electricity hums in my ears as the bunker fills with light.

Her husband's family must have taken Y2K extremely seriously. This is definitely no ordinary storm shelter. I'm expecting cracked wood and a tiny cube lit by a single light bulb, but instead I'm met by sleek walls and a ceiling covered in florescent light and vents. Madge catches me staring at them.

"They're wired normally, for now. The backup generator should keep them going for several months at least. The vents filter the air so we can keep things airtight."

"Oh," I say.

She's excited now, so she keeps going. The room we're in has nothing more than two bunk beds and shelves, but she turns down another hallway to reveal a kitchen.

"The doors are all completely sealed," she explains as she walks through one. "In case of cross contamination."

I keep nodding. It's inadvisable to let a crazy person know that you think they're crazy.

The kitchen contains a freezer, a fridge, and shelves and shelves of unboxed food. Madge turns on the sink and turns to me expectedly.

"It... works?" I guess.

She sighs. "We've got it on its own system, in case the plumbing gets contaminated. They only connect to our own water and waste tanks. We should have enough to last even longer than the lights."

"Cool." This clearly isn't just the work of some Y2K panic. It's a full on nuclear shelter. When we get back, I'm going to give Mr. Barber so much shit for not running a background check on the people he decided to send us to.

"Washroom's down the other hall," she continues. "If—"

"I'm sure I'll find it," I smile, putting a hand on her back to try and guide her back towards the ladder. "Thanks so much for the help."

"Wait!" She rushes through the kitchen and into a storage room, emerging with a pile of boxes literally labeled *Anti-Apocalypse Pills*. I'm trapped underground with a crazy person.

"Sorry dear," she smiles sympathetically. "Can't risk you kids taking these. They're the real deal."

"Right," I nod.

She frowns. "You can't go around telling people in town. On Tuesday everyone'll—"

"Our lips are sealed," I promise. "Trust me."

She squints at me because she doesn't.

"Well," she rubs her hands together. "Best be getting back to Roy. We'll be in the main house if you need anything."

"Right."

I dump out my bag, spread my papers out between the two bunks, and get studying.

Creepy old doomsday preppers or not, this tournament's mine.

Rory: 3 Years Before Impact

Mr. Barber rarely came to tournaments. He was a debate teacher because everyone expected the law teacher to take on that role, not because he enjoyed it. He always made a point of coming to the first away competition of the year though, just to trick the parents into thinking that he was responsible.

"Alright!" He declared the moment he'd shepherded us all off the bus. "I want to see everybody pair up!"

We all groaned or at least, I did. At fourteen, I was already convinced that I was an adult. I was ready to pair up with Lonny Church which would have made Barber happy anyway but then he said, "we'll be keeping the pairs for roommates at the hotel so same-sex matches please."

And instantly, I couldn't pair up with Lonny. Out of principle.

A few heads turned to me before I even raised my hand because I was very vocally out which meant that Mr. Barber should have realized that too. "Who do I pair up with?"

He sighed. We both knew the answer he wanted to give, but he stopped himself just in time. "Whichever gender you're feeling more like today."

It wasn't the first time an adult had suggested that as a solution and it wouldn't be the last. Not all nonbinary people were genderfluid. I didn't become more or less boy or girl day to day, I was always right in the middle.

"What the hell does—"

Finn's hand shot up. "I'll take Rory."

Her friends glared at her. So did Mr. Barber because there was a clear gender I was supposed to pair with, and it wasn't the one he was reading Finn as. "I'm not sure if—"

"Rory's gay," Finn subtly stepped on my foot, daring me to argue. "Nothing's going to happen."

Mr. Barber stared at Finn, did that thing that straight people do where they decide someone's sexuality based solely on how nice they perceive them to be, then nodded. "Great, thanks Finneas." He started leading us to the hotel.

"I'm not gay," I muttered.

Finn sighed. "Tell him you're pan and we'd be stuck there for hours while he tries to figure out what that means. Then has an aneurism when he realizes that not everyone's only attracted to one gender and there's actually no way to be absolutely sure he won't pair up two people who could potentially be into each other."

"I shouldn't have to lie about my identity just to appease—"

"Rory." She said. "Time and place. You have to pick and choose this shit."

I almost hit them. I would have, if I didn't think it would keep me from my first away tournament. Maybe I wouldn't have if I'd known that they were also queer, but I'd probably still at least want to.

"You're welcome," she said. "By the way."

That didn't make it any easier to keep myself from hitting her.

"Screw you. I didn't ask for help."

I ignored them all night, she ignored me all day, and we ended up staying together at every away tournament after that. They were right. It was a battle that I was too busy to fight.

Rory: 4 Days Before Projected Impact

"Holy shit."

By the time Finn lands in the bunker, I'm already nodding off. I shake myself awake, jumping to my feet.

"You okay?" I ask, thinking to sketchy ladders and a thin, dark descent.

They roll their eyes. "Stop doing that."

"You fell."

"Down like three rungs. I jumped. It was intentional."

"We can still get someone to switch," I remind her. "I'm sure—"

"I'm fine, Rory." They stop me. "Guarantee this place is bigger than any of the actual rooms would be anyway."

"No windows though," I point out. I'm extremely well versed in claustrophobia now. It's vital to know all of your partner's weaknesses inside and out to try and prevent any mishaps at tournaments. "Some people—"

"Believe it or not, you trying to list off all of the reasons I should be freaking out isn't going to help me not freak out."

"Oh," I say. 'Right."

"It's cute that you're so worried about me though," she smiles. "Almost sweet."

I roll my eyes. "I just don't need a panicky partner tomorrow."

"Sure."

She looks around. "This is insane."

"There are more rooms," I nod towards the kitchen.

"No shit?" She jogs off to go check.

I enjoy what I'm certain will be my last few moments of peace before they return.

"This is crazy impressive," Finn says.

"Or just crazy."

She shrugs. "Still awesome."

They sit down on the bunk closest to the kitchen's entrance. The one I'd been planning on claiming. They're identical though and not worth another argument right now, so I bite my tongue.

"You were out late," I observe instead, starting to sweep me notes back into a pile.

Finn nods. "Figured it was best to spend the least amount of time possible in a stranger's house. I don't know what Barber was thinking."

The worst thing—or at least, one of them—about Finn is that she used to be interesting. More annoying, sure, but at least interesting. When you got them mad, they'd come at you with deafening screams and clawing nails and meticulously thought through revenge plots. Now, she just keeps her distance and refused to admit that she's pissed. It's exceptionally harder to get even with someone pretending that they're not pissed. Maybe that's their newest form of revenge.

Since they're not acknowledging why they really spent all evening avoiding me, I don't either. "There was probably nothing else free," I acknowledge.

"That doesn't mean he couldn't have warned us!" She takes a deep breath, fiddles with her thumbs, and goes back to boring. "You're coming out with us tomorrow," they decide.

"Obviously. I didn't come all this way just to miss the tournament."

"I meant after."

I sigh. "Finn, I'll need to—"

"We can drop you off at a park or library or wherever so you can keep ignoring everyone. Whatever. I don't feel comfortable leaving you alone here for that long though. They seem... off."

I snort.

"What? I mean, even just having a bunker like this? That's weird, Rory."

"I know, I just didn't think you'd admit it. The old lady's like, obsessed with you."

They roll their eyes. "People actually like me. That doesn't mean they're not insane. You're staying out with us tomorrow, okay?"

I consider. "If I come, you let us prep for at least two hours Sunday morning."

"Jesus, Rory! I'm not bargaining with you over this!"

"Okay," I shrug. "Guess I'll stay here."

They sigh. "One hour."

"Deal." That's what I was going for anyway. Finn's painfully predictable.

We both go to sleep early the night before the tournament. Finn does it because I'm pretty sure they always do—she's the only person I know who actually tries to get the full 8-10 hours that teens are supposed to. I do because I get up at five every tournament day to go over things one last time. When I return from brushing my teeth, Finn's already under the blankets on their bottom bunk, facing the wall. Normally that works perfectly well for me, but I need to make sure that we don't go into tomorrow harbouring any grudges.

I climb to my top bunk. I'm not about to pass up one of my only opportunities to finally feel taller than her.

"Finn," I say.

They don't respond.

"Finn!"

"Sleeping," they grumble.

I roll my eyes. "You're obviously not. Talk to me for a sec or I start throwing things.

Slowly—and with a lot of overdramatic yawning and sighing considering that they must have only lied down a few minutes ago—she sits up. "What do you want, Rory?"

I'm suddenly deeply uncomfortable. I can apologize for a good cause, but it always feels worse with Finn.

"I'm sorry if I said anything stupid on the bus." I make sure I'm talking quickly. It'll make it end faster. That would be less awkward for both of us.

Finn doesn't seem to agree. "If?"

"Fine. Did, okay? I'm sorry that I did something stupid on the bus." I dangle my feet off the edge of the mattress. "I obviously know you're queer. I'm like, one of the only people at school who bothers getting your pronouns wrong."

They frown. "No one's been getting them wrong. It'd be pretty hard to."

"You know what I mean. Everyone else just uses he."

"You just use she/they."

"Because everyone else just uses he," I remind her. "I'm balancing things."

"I never asked you to do that."

"Yeah, well, you're welcome then I guess. There, now we're—"

"Is that why you don't think I'm actually queer?"

"I..." I scratch the back of my neck. "I was literally just saying that I hadn't meant that. Obviously. Just that like, in tournaments, it's more of a thing for me because I either let myself get mispronouned the entire round or have to let everyone in the room know that I'm nonbinary and have a personal stake in queer motions. You always just let people use he/him and then they get to assume that you're cis."

"I use any pronouns, Rory," she points out. "I can't get mad when people choose to stick with he/him."

"Right, but—"

"Is that why you never do? Because you think it makes me less queer if I still—"

I gape. "That's not... how the fuck did you land there? All of your friends only use he and they're fine, but I use two and I'm somehow what? Transphobic? I'm fucking trans!"

Finn sighs, squeezing the skin between their eyebrows. "There's nothing wrong with me not wanting to out myself every single round. I'm not going to random ask people to use different pronouns tomorrow just to impress you."

"Right, yeah. Obviously."

"There's also nothing wrong with 'he'. I like 'he'. Or... I don't, sometimes, but no more or less frequently than 'she' or 'they'. I'm not agender because I'm not a 'he', I'm agender because I'm all of it or none of it or... I don't know. But I'm equally all of it or none of it, I think. I'd still be the same me if I was assigned female so it's bullshit to say that I'm somehow less queer for still using 'he' but that 'she' would still be fine because it means you're obviously using my assigned gender as a prerequisite for how I'm allowed to identify."

"Okay," I nod. "Noted. Next time I complain about you I'll throw in a few 'he's and 'him's then."

"Good."

"You know that's not what I've been doing though, right? I've been using the way other people pronoun you to decide how I was going to, not your assigned gender. I know you're not–"

He sighs. "It's fine, Rory. You knew me way longer when I was identifying as a guy. That's obviously going to influence–"

"It doesn't though," I stop him. "I generally try to pretend you didn't exist pre-high school for the sake of my own sanity. I'm planning on blocking you out entirely once we graduate, actually."

The corner of his mouth ticks up. "Of course you are."

"We're fine then?" I check. "You know I wasn't... I apologized and explained so now we're done with it and you're not gonna be all pissy tomorrow, right?"

"We're as fine as always, I guess," he confirms. Then, a slow smile starts to creep across his face. And I know I'm screwed. "If–"

"You can't do that." I stop him. "You just said that we were fine."

"I'm unsaying it then. We're good if you stop doing that thing where you pretend you only care about people when they're useful to you and admit that you were apologizing because we're friends and you felt bad. No using tournaments as an excuse for being human."

I roll my eyes. "We're definitely not friends."

"Says the person who begged me to come across the province to compete with them."

"Because you're objectively good at debate. I apologized because I didn't want to self-sabotage myself for tomorrow and because I didn't want to feel like an asshole. That good enough?"

"Because we're friends and potentially hurting my feelings made you feel like an asshole?"

I just glare.

Finn sighs. "This is what? Our twenty somethingth tournament? The whole pretending you hate me thing got old in middle school, Rory."

I don't even know why I'm entertaining this. I've done my part and he's obviously bluffing. Finn would never lose on purpose.

"Get some sleep," I slide under my covers, rolling to face the opposite wall. "Big day tomorrow."

"You're such a dick."

"Takes one to know one. Night."

Finn sighs. I hear shuffling, the light goes off, and we're plunged into total darkness.

Things feel unfinished, so I add, "sweet dreams."

"Fuck off."

That must have been the issue. I sleep like a baby.

Rory: 3 Days Before Projected Impact

For a moment, I truly believe that Finn must have been impossibly correct. Some part of me–some deep, repressed, insufferable part of me–must be freaking out about him freaking out because while I wake unable to remember what I was dreaming about, it must cling to me. I jolt awake to the ground shaking.

But then, once I'm fully conscious, it takes too long to stop.

I roll over to find Finn pacing the gap between our bunks, a black box I don't recognize clutched between her hands. As the shaking subsides, I notice my belongings. Someone's opened my bag and my clothes, notes, snacks, and toiletries are strewn across the ground.

I rub at my eyes, sitting up. "What the fuck did–"

Their attention snaps to me. "Where's your phone?"

"What?"

"Where's your fucking phone, Rory?"

I reach into my pillowcase for it. "Calm down. It's just–"

She drops the box onto her bed and holds out her hands. "Pass it."

"What? No, I'm not–"

Finn sighs, getting back to pacing. Their hair's disheveled and their eyes are red and buggy, but I can't tell if it's from sleep or whatever he's freaking out about now. "Call someone, okay? Can you call someone?"

I decide to humour her. Maybe then we can go back to sleep for a bit longer. When I click on my screen, it reads 4:07. I sigh. "It's like, 4am. No one's–"

"They don't have to pick up. I just... check if it goes through?"

I click on Alice's contact. If she wants me to play nice with Finn Williams, then she gets to deal with getting woken up in the middle of the night for him.

"Shit," I say after two failed attempts. "I don't have service. But we're in a freaky bunker so—"

"We did last night though."

"Maybe it's spotty. We're in the middle of farmland. I'm sure it'll be back soon."

They abruptly stop moving to stare at me. "You heard that too, right? You felt that?"

I frown. "I didn't hear anything."

"Don't fuck with me right now Rory! Don't... I can't deal with that right now."

"I didn't hear anything," I repeat slowly. "I felt the shaking, but it could have just been an earthquake."

"Service went out a bit ago," he rambles. "I found this radio thing in the storage closet and every channel was talking about the asteroid and then there's this huge noise and everything goes fucking silent."

I shrug. "Maybe the earthquake downed a few powerlines."

"Service, wifi, and radio feeds?"

"I'm..." for half a second, something spikes in my chest. I remind myself that it's 4am. I'm tired. I'm feeding off of Finn's paranoia. We have more pressing things than apocalypses to worry about, so I take two long breaths and try to logic my way through it. "Maybe connections are spotty down here. We are, you know, underground and all? The asteroid wasn't even supposed to hit for a few more days." I hop off the bunk. "I'll open the hatch, we'll step out for a few seconds, and then we'll like, march you to the farmhouse and you can crash on someone's floor, okay? Or even probably on the plastic couches. The owner's obsessed with you, I'm sure she won't mind. We don't need to be dealing with all of this right now."

I get up five rungs before he tugs on my leg, almost making me lose my footing. "What the fuck?" I focus on keeping both of my hands on the bar, kicking in her general direction.

"You can't open it. The air can be dangerous. They were saying that it might—"

I roll my eyes. "I'm sure I'll survive. I'll just—"

"You can't open it!" Finn screams.

I squeeze my eyes shut and take two more long breaths. It's too early to be dealing with any of this.

"Okay," I relent, hopping back down and raising my hands in surrender. "We give it until eight and see if service is back. I'm not missing this tournament just because you've freaked yourself out though, okay? You've got four-ish hours to calm down."

They nod. "Thank you."

I'll check when they fall back asleep, of course. He'll thank me for it when he wakes up. Finn's just being paranoid.

"I'm getting back to sleep," I announce, pulling myself back up onto my top bunk. "You should do the same."

But she doesn't. They pace and mutter and keep clicking the buttons on that stupid fucking radio so repetitively that I'm convinced I'll have what each and every one of them sounds like memorized for the rest of my life. Maybe his feet finally get tired at some point because when I give in and crack my eyes open, Finn's sitting in the middle of their bottom bunk, legs pulled to his chest.

"Okay," I sigh, hopping back down. This, at least, I know how to fix. I walk past their bed and fill a metal cup with water from the tap in the kitchen. I don't exactly trust the cleanliness of a self-contained system set up by a bunch of paranoid men decades ago, but it's the best I have to work with. When I return, Finn's still curled in on themselves, breathing heavily. Sweat plasters his bangs to his forehead.

"Here," I sit down beside them, holding out the water. "Drink."

"I don't–"

"You're sweating which means you're losing fluid and you're hyperventilating which means you'd probably already be dizzy without also factoring in potential dehydration. Drink."

She accepts the cup and takes a few sips. His hand shakes so severely that water sloshes over the rim. I shouldn't have filled it so high.

When they seem finished, I take the cup back to prevent further spillage. I place it down on the floor and lean back against the wall.

"You need to slow down your breathing too, yeah? Doing it this quickly definitely isn't helping."

Finn glares. "I can't.... just..."

"I know," I hold out my hands at stare at him until he reluctantly places his fingers on top of me. "We'll do it together, alright? When I bring our hands up, breath in through your nose. When we go down, exhale through your mouth. It's supposed to be the best way to signal to your body that it needs to stop being annoying. Don't remember why, but trying's probably better than depriving your brain of oxygen, right? Ready?"

They don't respond.

"Finn." I squeeze her fingers. "You ready?"

He nods once, so I start. His eyes flutter shut as we work, but I've anticipated that already and worked around it with the physical contact. When their breaking isn't audibly fucked up anymore, I adjust my grip and pinch the skin between their thumb and forefinger.

"Ow!" She pulls away, clutching their hand to her chest. Their eyes burst open. "What the fuck, Rory!"

I shrug. "Sudden physical changes are supposed to be good for grounding people. Most sites suggest using ice cubes, but I'm pretty sure we don't have access to any of those right now. I improvised."

"I'm pretty sure most sites don't suggest inflicting bodily harm!"

"I told you, I was improvising," I remind him. "Stop being such a baby, I barely touched you. You'll survive."

Their fingers dart out to pinch my arm, but I catch them with my other hand. It feels stranger, somehow, now that she's calmed down. My brain's been at peak function this whole time, but once I know that his is too, their fingers make mine feel fuzzy. I think I might be allergic to Finn Williams.

I swallow, quickly letting go. "Don't think I won't retaliate if you try to attack me again later."

She laughs a little, but it's forced. "I'm sure you will."

"You're okay now, right?"

Finn raises an eyebrow. "Ready to admit that you're checking because you care about me?"

I roll my eyes. "I care about making sure your brain's getting enough oxygen, stupid." I tap the side of her head. "That's the only part of you that's useful to me."

"My brain will survive then."

"Good." I nod. "We have a tournament in a few hours. Get some sleep."

They frown. "Rory, I can't just–"

"Nope," I stop her. "I agreed to your thing, so we're doing mine, okay? When service comes back in a few hours or someone comes to collect us and tell us that the power went out, we're going to be well rested."

He's quiet. His eyes flicker to the ladder then back to me. "Okay," she says. "Fine."

I climb back up my bunk and close my eyes, listening for the exact moment when their breathing regulates. Once it does, I quietly climb down again. I'll push open the hatch, leave it propped up, and when Finn wakes, he'll have to admit that he was just being a paranoid idiot. But before I even make it past the first rung of the ladder, I check my phone again.

4:52. Still no service.

I sigh and return to my bunk. It's not like we'd be able to go anywhere right now anyway and if nothing's going on—which it isn't—then someone really will get in contact with us soon.

I'm not worried, I'm just practical. Logical. I don't give in to hairbrained conspiracy theories just because they got lucky enough to line up with an actual earthquake. I'm just trying to avoid giving my debate partner another reason to be mad at me.

Rory: 4 Years Before Impact

Finn Williams broke a girl's heart in grade eight. She wasn't a friend. We'd all known each other since kindergarten, so it would be physically impossible for someone to be friends with one of us while crushing on the other.

The whole set up was elaborate. Very Finn. Jenny got all of her friends to trick them into some Pictionary-charades crossover, manipulated Finn into the middle of the circle, and then had them all turn their boards around to reveal messages of *J+F at grad?*

It was extremely progressive of Jenny and the perfect level of cheesiness for Finn so when I found out that they'd apparently laughed, pushed their way through the circle, and immediately went to go tell their friends about it presumably to laugh some more, I struck.

Jenny was not my friend, but Finn was my enemy. That was what mattered.

She knew it was coming too. Everyone did. The moment one of her friends caught sight of me they started chanting "fight, fight, fight!"

We'd never fought physically before. Yet, somehow, we both decided that it was time to in the same moment. I don't know who started it, but we were rolling and screaming and tugging and hitting—albeit half-heartedly. Me: because I didn't want to risk suspension, Finn: probably for similar reasons—until a teacher split us up and sent us to the principal's office.

We were sat down. We were asked what had happened and I made the mistake of saying "He broke Jenny H.'s heart," which made it sound like I'd instigated things even though I still was pretty sure that I hadn't.

The principal sighed, already making up her mind. Maybe she had the moment we'd walked in. By all accounts, she was supposed to side with me. Finn was taller, more physically fit, popular, and someone that she thought was a boy. I was a small, pale, mousy ghost of something that she thought was a girl. But Finn was already on his public image kick, so she turned to them.

"Did she start it?"

"They," we corrected in tandem.

"no one started it. It just... happened," I added.

She sighed. "I don't want to get both of you in trouble right before graduation."

Finn was supposed to give a speech. I was supposed to give nothing. Suddenly, I was incredibly okay with us both getting in trouble.

"Neither of you seem hurt. Maybe we could—"

"I'll tell my parents," I said.

Finn kicked my leg. I hoped the principal caught it.

"We should both be held accountable. I don't think they'll be too happy if they see they kid who attacked me talking about how supportive of a community we are next week."

Finn kicked my leg again.

The principal frowned. "You either both get in trouble or we can all just agree to call this an accident."

"It wasn't an accident." It wasn't entirely malicious either, but I would have said anything to get her blamed. I would always remember that Finn was willing to destroy themself to get to me. I always had to be ready to do the same.

The principal turned to Finn. "If—"

She used the wrong name so, in tandem again, we both said, "Rory."

The principal beamed, looking at me and waiting for me to do the same. As if Finn was some kind of saint for knowing the name I'd been using for months already by that point. "Are you sure we can't just let this go, Rory?" She said it with emphasis. She said it like I was a four-year-old who'd just insisted that she call me Batman. "Finneas seems willing to compromise. Maybe we could—"

"I never said that," Finn interrupted. "Rory attacked me."

"Liar."

"Bigger liar."

She adjusted her glasses. We were occasionally a tiring duo. "You seem like good kids," she told Finn. "Respectful kids," she emphasized for me. "I'm sure—"

"Finneas isn't a better person than me just because he knows my name. I know his too."

She sighed. "Rory," again, the emphasis. Again, the condescension. "You know that's not the same thing, dear."

The bell rang. Finn got up. "We'd better get to class."

"First we have to—"

"Give someone else the speech. Give us lunch time detention or a suspension or something. They're not going to change their mind and we have a test." We didn't have a test.

"Finneas!" I followed them out.

He glared, spinning around. "You gonna attack me again?"

"You started it."

"Maybe," she sighed, fingers tapping at her side, heels bouncing against the floor. "That was stupid. We can't keep doing stuff like that at school."

I nodded.

"Do you think they told them yet?" He asked. "Our parents?"

"In the last two seconds? No."

She nodded and kept nodding. I'd known them long enough to recognize them getting caught in an action when they were freaking out. I sighed. "I'll tell Ms. L you'll be late."

He kept nodding. I winced, hating the words more in my head than out loud.

"This was stupid," I admitted. "I'll go say we changed our minds. I'm sure she hasn't told anyone yet."

They kept nodding.

"Finneas. Nothing's official yet, okay? Stop being weird."

They nodded one final time. "I'll probably still be late to class."

"Well now I will be too, so you're on your own with that one."

Rory: 3 Days Before Impact

"It's not eight o'clock yet."

I got back up at six to keep preparing. I have less time to study than I was planning on now, but I also didn't want to risk exhaustion.

Finn got back up at six thirty to keep pacing.

A list of more accurate words to describe Finn Williams than 'nice': bouncy, loud, claustrophobic, in motion.

I check my phone for the twelfth time in the last ten minutes. She's horribly distracting. "It will be in seven more minutes."

"We can still wait for someone to come."

"Finn."

"We can wait!"

I stop collecting my notes to rub at my eyes. "We agreed I'd open it at eight."

"I know, but—"

"You get you're being paranoid, right? The danger's all in your head so once we open it up and show your body that it doesn't actually have anything to worry about, you'll feel fine again."

Her fingers tap against her jeans. "I know, but it doesn't... you can't open it. If I'm right, you can't—"

I sigh for the billionth time this morning. I should have opened the hatch when I'd had the chance to while she was asleep. Now, they're using their annoyingly tall frame to block access to the ladder.

"Fine." I throw up my arms, pretending to give in. "We'll wait a bit longer. But if we had to skip breakfast to get there on time, I'm not letting you share my snacks." Finn never packs enough for herself. They're used to other people just giving them things.

His shoulders relax. "Thank you."

I wait for Finn to sit down before making a break for the ladder.

"Rory!" She's taller—and honestly, probably faster—but I somehow get halfway up before Finn grabs onto my leg.

I shake my foot, but they hold tight.

"You couldn't wait five more minutes?"

"You're not going to let me open it in five minutes either!"

He doesn't contest that. We both know that I'm right.

"If it was just an earthquake, it was a huge one," she says. "They probably postponed it anyway. Getting to a tournament isn't worth risking fucking radiation poisoning!"

That right there is all the proof I need that I shouldn't have depended on her in the first place. Finn's good at debate, but she's never cared about it enough.

"Let go."

"No."

"Let go!"

My leg finally breaks free. I feel it connect with something and then suddenly, they're letting go of my other ankle as well.

"Rory!"

I move up one rung. Another.

"I swear to god, Rory, open that hatch and I won't come! You won't even be able to compete!"

I hesitate. Not because they're right, of course. I'm sure I could spook one of the younger kids about the asteroid enough to get them to drop out to hide away with Finn while I steal their partner.

But we wouldn't do as well.

So, I hesitate. Not because I believe him, I just do. I make the mistake of looking down and she has a hand cupped around her mouth and her eyes are wide and she's screaming at me, but she doesn't look angry. She looks terrified. I sigh and descend. Injuring and emotionally scarring everyone's favourite exec won't help my search for a replacement partner.

Finn watches me. "Thank you."

"Shut up," I say. "There's still time left so I'm gonna keep being annoying and get you to snap out of whatever the fuck this is. This isn't you winning."

She nods because of course, she knew that already.

"Move your hand." I instruct. "Are you hurt? Do you need... I don't know. Mysterious doomsday prepper freezer stuff?"

"Maybe?"

I go off in search of it. The freezer, apparently, is currently just being used as an extra storage space for things that don't actually require freezing. I grab an aluminum tin of instant coffee and return to the bedroom.

"Here." I hand him the can, sitting down beside her. They're trembling, but their lip hasn't even started swelling yet, so I don't have to worry about it being from blood loss.

They press the can against their lower lip. "If everything's fine up there, they'll probably come collect us before they leave."

I nod. "I know."

"It makes sense to wait it out. It's the most logical—"

"Both paranoia and anxiety are typically characterized by irrational or illogical thoughts."

His freehand flies to my wrist.

I roll my eyes. "I'm not about to try and run for it again. You're useless to me all angry and bleedy. I just like correcting people."

They let go, but their fingers remain millimeters from mine. She doesn't trust me. That's fine, they probably shouldn't.

"I didn't mean to bust your lip open," I admit.

Finn nods. "I know."

"It could distract the judges."

They roll their eyes. "You're ridiculous."

"Says the person refusing to let me open a door because of an earthquake and his inability to get service. Several meters underground."

"We'll still make the tournament," she says.

"We'd better."

Finn takes a deep breath. It makes his shoulders shake. "If they don't come and get us before it'd be too late, I don't think I can–"

"If they don't and we miss it, you'll owe me forever. That's practically as good as winning," I lie.

She stands up and claps, but it's devoid of its usual energy. I'm not sure how long they were up last night. "I guess we might as well check out your notes."

Rory: 3 Days Before Projected Impact

No one comes before the tournament starts at 10:00. Not any of the team or Madge or her weird alien loving husband. Finn does an awful job at hiding my phone from me near 9:30, but I pretend not to notice. It's not like thirty minutes would be enough time to get there anyway.

She hands it back at 10:16. She says, "I'm sorry."

I still don't have any service or wifi. I reply, "fuck off," climb back onto the top bunk, and stare at the wall.

That's all it takes. Sixteen minutes and the worst timed earthquake and service outage ever and suddenly the last four years of my life were all for nothing. Finn will be fine. Finn does debate because he's insufferably, annoyingly, naturally good at it. Finn's going to grow up and do acting or film production or something equally artsy and probably didn't even mention being president of the debate team on most of their university applications to save space for all the productions and acting workshops they were a part of.

My whole life is debate. My whole life is going to be debate. It never makes sense to other people but when student athletes tie their whole identities to their sports, that's considered normal. People like Finn get to revolve everything around whatever show's currently in production and no one bats an eye. I've known since I was nine that I was going to be a fantastic high school debater then a fantastic university debater then a fantastic lawyer. Logically I know that I can still do the rest of that without ever making it to provincials, let alone placing at nations, but if I couldn't even get that close in a sea of mediocrity, what does that say about me?

I hear the constant rhythm of Finn's pacing, but every time they say anything their voice is semi-stable, so I keep myself wrapped up in my little blanket cocoon of sadness and ignore them.

As time ticks by and I'm sure the first day of the tournament must be over, I start to feel their paranoia take root at the back of my brain. The team should have realized that we were missing and come to check on us by now. Maybe they're out to dinner and will soon. Maybe Madge and her husband are actually axe wielding murderers and they're coming to get us next.

Axe murders are much more manageable than apocalypses, so I decide to go for that and mourn the team's lost potential all on my own because the moment I let myself talk to Finn, her paranoia will permanently infect me.

"Rory," they say.

I've been ignoring it all day, so it's easy to pretend to be asleep the thousandth time she tries to get my attention.

"Can I steal some of your snacks?"

I'd pretend to start snoring if I didn't know that that'd give me away.

"Keep ignoring me and I'm taking your silence as a yes."

I sigh, rolling over. "Silence almost never means yes, for the record."

He's sitting on his bottom bunk, grinning up at me. He knew that already. "I need something to eat."

"Go outside and get something then." I'm not getting her to test the air first because I'm afraid of it. I'm just heroically giving her a head start on escaping the axe murderers.

Finn doesn't respond.

I roll my eyes. "The place is full of food. Go take some."

"I can't just steal!"

"If you're right, they're all dead, right? It won't matter." I roll back over. A few seconds later, I hear them get up.

"It's eight," Finn says when she returns from wherever he went to go steal from.

I don't respond.

"Rory. Stop doing that. I obviously know you're awake."

"Maybe I just don't want to talk to you."

Sighing and shuffling and then suddenly my mattress is shifting. I bolt up to find Finn sitting cross-legged right beside the ladder.

I glare. "We've established that I'm not against knocking you off of things."

"That was an accident."

"Maybe."

They tilt their head back. "It's eight pm."

"I know."

"No one's come yet. They must've noticed we're missing but they didn't–"

"I know." Pesky axe murderers.

"Maybe you should pop over to the farmhouse and make sure everything's okay."

I go cold. I'm pretty sure Finn "nicest person in the fucking universe" Williams is trying to get me to sacrifice myself to what they're convinced is a toxic wasteland. I'd technically done the same, but I'm still holding out for axe murderers and besides, it's at least on brand for me. "Holy shit."

"Obviously I was just being paranoid earlier, but if they haven't come to check on us, they might be–"

"You go check," I stop him.

"If you want," she shrugs. "Just figured you'd want to since you were so eager to get out of here earlier."

"I'm fine crashing here. They like you more anyway."

She doesn't move. Because I'm right.

"Holy shit! You were going to let me expose myself to weird space toxins. Just like that!"

He blushes. "I mean... you don't believe in it, so..."

"You still do! You go out."

"I... no."

"I'm not either."

Finn nods. "We can just wait until tomorrow. It's not like they'd go home without us, right?"

"Fine. Whatever. I'm keeping my snacks."

She sucks on her lip for a moment. "Just so you know, I would have been like, super sad if you choked to death on deadly space toxins."

I roll my eyes. "Then I guess we're stuck here until I get to tell everyone how stupid you're being tomorrow morning."

Rory: 9 Years Before Impact

Finn put gum in my hair when I was eight. When everyone else rewrites our history to make him the tragic victim, they always leave that kind of thing out. It was up high, just beneath my ear. We had to cut it down to basically the length I like to keep it at now anyway, but as an eight-year-old, it was devastating. My hair never came back quite as blonde, and my parents mourned it for months.

Finn put gum in my hair but somehow, everyone always frames her as the good one.

Rory: Day 3 In the Bunker

The next day passes in silence. No one comes.

"Rory," Finn says.

I ignore them. I've spent the whole day reading my notes, even though they're useless now. Research is my happy place.

"We were supposed to leave by now."

"I know."

"I think something's probably really, really, wrong."

"I know." I don't look up from my duotang. Me spiralling too would not be productive. In my peripherals, I see them look towards the ladder. I resist the urge to do the same.

I lick my lips. "If they're already gone it's not like there's any rush, right? They were talking about closing school Monday and Tuesday because of how many parents were complaining. We'll wait until the owners kick us out."

"Okay, sure."

They will, of course. There's no way they won't want the bunker for themselves come Tuesday.

Rory: Day 5 in the Bunker

Tuesday comes. Tuesday goes. All that remains is me, Finn, and a world of metal.

Rory: Day 6 in the Bunker

The world is supposed to end with a bang. If you ask Finn, it did. He keeps rambling about some sound that she's convinced must have woken me up Saturday morning that I'm convinced that she must have just imagined.

When I ask them to describe it, they say it was "too loud to hear," which is oxymoronic and just gives me more proof that they imagined it.

The world is supposed to end with a bang and there was no bag so this cannot be the end of the world. The end of the world is supposed to happen decades after I've left it, so this is not allowed to be the end of the world.

Logical fallacies are only valid when I control them.

The farmhouse caught on fire and no one knows where we are. We imagined there being service on our first night here and that's why it hasn't come back. It just never existed in the first place.

This is not the end of the world. It's a smaller disaster. A different disaster. One that won't affect my life anymore once Finn grows up, opens the hatch, and proves to both of us that everything's fine. We'll go home and Alice will make fun of me for all of eternity and Finn will go on some talk show to make jokes about it.

They're the one who got us all paranoid. We would be gone already if he hadn't freaked out Saturday morning. It's only fair that they also be the first one to risk leaving.

Rory: Day 7 in the Bunker

If this is the end of the world, then Finn's better at it than me.

That disgusts me.

They boil large portions of rice in the smallest amounts of water possible and pass a serving up to my bunk twice a day then conserve the water to use again the next time they need it. I stay in my bunk all day but he, predictably, is always in motion. If she's not reading some of the old, bent books from the small selection in the storage room, Finn's doing push ups or jogging laps. They're a good apocalypse person.

"Can you fucking stop it?" I finally explode the third time they go through their workout routine in less than an hour. "We're not going to have to fight zombies. What the fuck are you training for?"

She shrugs, blowing her bangs out of her eyes. "It's important to keep our brains and bodies active."

"It's also incredibly annoying."

She just shrugs again, so I roll back over and reopen my notes.

And then the jumping restarts.

"I told you to fucking stop it!" I chuck the duotang towards her before I can process what I'm doing. It gets less than two feet away from the edge of the bunk before plummeting towards the ground.

My hands shake as I raise them to cover my mouth. "I... I'm sorry. I don't know why—I'm sorry."

Finn frowns, scooping up the folder. "Rory, it didn't—"

"I'm sorry," I repeat. "I didn't mean to... I didn't—"

"Rory." They pop up onto their toes to hand me the folder. "it didn't even come close to hit me."

I try to take the duotang back, but my fingers aren't working well enough to do it. "I'm sorry," I say again. Because I can't grab the folder.

"I'm coming up, okay?" he declares. "No pushing."

I'm not sure my arms would even if I wanted them to.

"There." She slips the duotang back into my bag where it belongs. But then she doesn't leave. "You doing okay?"

Of course I am. Finn's the one who's a mess. They've only been functioning this well these last couple of days to distract themself from it.

I lick my lips to unstick them, but then decide to just nod.

"Okay. Promise not to tell anyone if you're not though. You have way more dirt on me anyway."

I roll my eyes. It must shake a tear lose, because suddenly I'm sobbing. Not even for good reasons. Not for my parents who I liked well enough or my grandparents who I loved or Alice who I somethinged. For me. Because I'm stuck in a stupid fucking bunker.

Finn waits, silent and still. Until her body forgets that it's never supposed to be either of those things and suddenly her arms are wrapped around me. The shock is enough to force me to get control of my crying.

"What are you doing?" I demand.

"Hugging you. Like most people do when people start crying around them?"

"Well stop it," I shake off their arms. "That's gross."

They roll their eyes and lean back against the wall. "Knew you were scared."

"I'm not scared, I'm frustrated," I defend myself. I fold my arms over my chest. "This much time alone with you would make anyone frustrated."

"Most people actually like me a lot more than you pretend not to."

"Sure."

They sigh, looking towards the hatch. "One of us needs to open it eventually. Just to know for sure and keep us from going insane."

"Well, I'm not doing it."

"Me either." He thinks for a moment. "Do you have a coin in your bag?"

"Obviously."

"Let's flip for it."

I roll my eyes. "We're not flipping over who has to potentially breath in toxic dust."

"You have any better ideas?"

I sigh, fishing around in the side pocket of my bag for a loonie. I don't ask Finn which side she wants. They're always tails, I'm always heads.

"No cheating," he says.

"Yeah. Obviously."

We watch it flip. I catch it in the air and slam it against the back of my hand.

I wait as long as I can before lifting my fingers up, because I think I must somehow already know.

We lean over to stare at the loonie and then at each other.

"Rory..." she starts. I don't need this. I don't need them to play sweet, sympathetic, popular kid right after signing me up for what they're convinced might be a suicide mission.

"Shut up." I don't feel like pushing past them to climb down the bunk, so I just jump. I walk to the base of the ladder.

Finn hovers a few feet away, hands in his pocket. "You don't..." she doesn't finish the sentence, because there's no right way to end it. One of us has to, and it's apparently me. The coin gods have chosen.

If I'm about to die for Finn Williams, I'm not going to let them be all sappy about it.

She sways from foot to foot near the bottom of the ladder.

I sigh. "You can run away, you know."

His eyes widen because he somehow still hasn't realized how readable he is. "I wasn't..."

"The doors all seal, apparently. If I'm about to let in some kind of deadly toxin or carcinogen or instantly human frying light or something, it's stupid to be here too."

She nods once. "See you in a second?'

"Sure."

I watch him disappear into the kitchen and wait for them to close the door.

And then, I don't climb.

I like to think of myself as a logical person. It's my best asset. One of us has to open the hatch eventually, and that one of us is apparently going to be me. Standing here waiting is pointless because I have no use for a few more minutes of throat-clogging anxiety. Humans are not built to be logical, though. We spent too long evolving in realities far too different from the rapidly changing modern world to be. My body has never hunted or survived the harsh outdoors or really ever had to fight for its life in any way, but despite there being no logical better option, it refuses to climb. My palms slick and my muscles shake because they're expecting me to go along with them.

I remind myself that I'm being stupid and paranoid but I am a logical person and we're fairly hard to trick. So, when my brain finally regains enough control to move to the ladder, I'm no more eager to reach the top. Maybe I never would, if I didn't know that there was someone waiting a room over to witness my failure. Maybe it still would be impossible if that person wasn't Finn Williams who definitely, under no circumstances, is allowed to see me as a coward.

I reach the top. I touch the underside of the metal and it feels cool, not hot. I tell myself that that's a good sign despite the ever-present AC and vague memories of hearing that some hypothesize that a large enough asteroid would kickstart an impact winter. Surely it would take more time for that to set in.

The hatch isn't locked because we had no reason to lock it. I was hoping that it would be. Then, maybe, I could open it thinking that someone had come for us. Multiple someones. That they just hadn't been able to reach us because of our own stupidity.

When I push the hatch, it's heavy, but it's also metal. That's to be expected.

Then, I can't see. There's ash or dirt or dust or something in my nostrils, eyes, ears, and mouth. I wrap my arms around the ladder's top rung to keep myself from falling as I try to cough it back out, but it feels fused to my throat. I cup hands around my eyes and blink. This is proof of nothing. We're underground, after all. Maybe dirt shifted or Madge came back to cover us up and let us slowly waste away to conceal her murderous tendencies. I blindly push up against the ground to try and get above it, but even as my vision clears slightly, I still can't see. We're not buried. Or if we were, it was only slightly and I'm above it now. I don't have to dig through dirt, but there's only browns and whites and grays as far as my faulty vision can see. It stings my eyes and ears and throat and soul so after waiting a few more moments in case things miraculously clear up, I push myself back through the hatch and close it as quickly as I can. Blindly, I feel my way down to the ground and let myself fall to the floor in a coughing heap.

I don't hear Finn talking until I've regained most control of my senses, but there's a good chance they have been the whole time.

"Rory!" They yell, still safely hidden behind the door.

I groan and force myself to get up and move closer to it. My insides feel raw. I don't think I'd be able to yell right now. "I'm back," I say.

"What did... I'm guessing it's not good?"

"Just dust," I report. "Too thick to see anything. And pretty much like, physically fused to me for all of eternity now."

"Shit," Finn says. "Shit."

And then, they walk away.

Rory: 2 Years Before Impact

I'd had plenty of opportunities to throw Finn Williams under the bus over the years, but never more than right after they came out in tenth grade. She did it just late enough that everyone had decided that I was the upmost authority in their lives on all things genderqueer. I've never been more popular than right after she came out.

I got a lot of "isn't he offensive?"s and "doesn't he just piss you off?"s. The answer to both was yes for entirely non-gender related reasons, but I said no every time anyway because I knew it would be misconstrued if I answered with anything closer to honesty.

I'd had plenty of opportunities to throw Finn under the bus over the years but even though they're the good one so I'm supposed to be the bad one by default, I've never done it when it actually mattered.

Rory: Day 7 in the Bunker

"Finn!" I slam my palm against metal. "Open the fucking door!"

I'm an idiot. I should have lied. It would have been so easy to lie.

'Everything's fine! Come out and away from literally all the food and supplies please!'

And yet, I told the person that I knew was already paranoid about mysterious space diseases before we'd even gotten proof that anything was going on that I'd been contaminated.

After urging them to seal themself away with the food.

"Finn!" I wack the door again. My throat still aches, but I'll scream until it stops working altogether. "The bathroom's on my side, asshole! You can't just hide in there forever!"

Except that she could. Maybe disgustingly, but she has food and supplies and a sink and a stove and maybe he's decided that that'll be enough. I have a washroom, beds, and the bit of junk food left in my bag.

I kick the door. I don't remember until after I've already made contact that you're not supposed to kick things straight on. I hop back swearing and stumble onto his bed as a wave of pain and nausea overcomes me. It's my own fault. I would have done the exact same thing. But despite how much I try to remind myself that Finn's nice, selfless, 'friend to everyone' persona is fake, I fell for it when it mattered most.

If I am going to die here, I'll scream until the moment my lungs can't anymore. I'll hit and kick and curse. If I am going to die here, my final act will be making Finn Williams's life as inconvenient as possible.

And then, the door opens. Finn emerges, metal cup in hand.

"You're a mess."

I'm too exhausted and terrified and shellshocked to respond, so I just look up and glare.

"My bed too? Seriously Rory? You couldn't fuck up your own sheets?"

"It was the closest," I croak.

She sighs, sitting down beside me. He hands me the cup. I take slow, small sips. I want to savour my throat coming back to life. And procrastinate talking to them.

"You heard me?" I check.

She nods.

"You could've responded, you know."

"I did. You were being too loud though and I didn't feel like straining my voice."

I say nothing.

"The door wasn't even locked, Rory. I wouldn't–"

I know. That's why told them to get behind it. I already knew. "I would've."

"I know." He leans back. "Luckily for you, I'm not you though, huh?"

I nod at the dust or ash or dirt or space debris beneath their palms. "If I'm contaminated with something, you are too now. There's no point trying–"

Finn sighs. "Yes, Rory. I'm aware."

I pull my knees to my chest. Brush gray off of my pants. "I don't hate you, for the record. Or... not in the want you to die way. It just... we both know it would have been the logical choice. That's why only one of us went up. It would have been nothing personal."

She just nods.

"Why?" I ask. I don't have to elaborate.

They just shrug. "It's the end of the world, right? Who'd want to spend it alone?"

Rory: Day 7 In the Bunker

I take a shower. I take too long of a shower for someone who should be conserving water but no matter how clean my skin appears to be or how raw I rub it, it won't stop itching. I am not sick. I can't be sick because surely that would take longer to set in. There aren't any blisters or rashes because it's just dust and I'm fine. I'm just anxious. Anxiety can make you imagine sensations that aren't really there.

Still, once I force myself to get out, my skin's still buzzing. I check myself over in the mirror four times before getting dressed and returning to the main room. Finn's confiscated my old clothes and sealed them away somewhere. The only alternative outfit I brought was too formal, so I have to double knot the too big sweatpants that they found in storage just to keep them up.

Finn's been conserving water like crazy and reminded me that we'd have to just drain my shower water instead because of potential contaminants three separate times before letting me wash off, so I ready myself for her to yell at me for staying in too long. Maybe I want them to. Instead, I open the door to find him sorting out puzzle pieces between our beds. She looks up. She's washed her hair once since getting here, but it's already getting greasy again. A clump hits their forehead. "You good?"

I nod wordlessly because obviously, we're both anything but.

Finn returns their attention to the puzzle. I carefully step around it to climb back up to my bunk.

"You can help," he stops me. "I'm not really a puzzle person, but I found it in storage and figured we'd need something to keep us busy."

"Until what? We run out of food and water?"

They shrug. "Beats dying of starvation, dehydration, and boredom, right? Do the puzzle."

I stare. "Why are you so okay with this?"

"I'm not. But I've been pretty sure we were fucked for a week now. It'll get boring spending all of your time wallowing in it. Trust me. Do the puzzle."

"We're going to die, Finn." I remind them. "Everyone else probably already did."

"So, there's nothing keeping you from puzzling then."

"Finn."

She sighs. "Would you rather die quiet or die living? I know my answer."

"The one that isn't an oxymoron. And requires a lot less effort on my part."

"You're so full of shit."

"Maybe—"

"You want to live, Rory. You wouldn't have started screaming at me if you didn't want to live."

I roll my eyes. "Maybe I was just mad."

"No, you were scared."

"Maybe I was just worried that I wouldn't outlive you then. That'd mean that you'd get the final win."

"Well?" He waves an arm over his puzzle pieces. "Come outlive me then."

We do their stupid puzzle.

Rory: Day 7 in the Bunker

"What do you think happened to them?" I call while Finn's in the kitchen working on dinner. I'm better at talking to her when we're in different rooms. "Everyone else?"

"When a giant space rock hit? They probably died. Even if they weren't directly where it landed it would have fucked up the whole atmosphere."

"There are probably other people camping out in some places. In things like this."

"Yup." I listen to pots clang. "Billionaires, conspiracy theorists, world leaders, and us."

"Did you know anyone with a plan? Your family or friends or... anyone?"

He's quiet. Then, the clanging starts up again. "I don't think there was a single bunker in our entire town, Rory."

"Right," I say. "Right."

I roll onto my other side and leave them alone.

Rory: 2 Years Before Impact

I'd always known that despite the general public seeming to think otherwise, Finn coming out had nothing to do with me.

Doing it so close to a tournament then missing five days of school as a result had to be an attempt to spite me though.

I texted and Instagram messaged and even emailed them a million "hey"s and demands to meet up to practice. It wasn't until I threatened to show up at her house that he knocked on my door.

"You still have to do the tournament," I informed them.

She sighed. "I wasn't planning on bailing."

"Good." I led the way to my basement. She followed. I knew that he would.

"What have people been saying?" He asked.

A lot. "I tend to try my best not to listen to other people. Especially when they're talking about you."

"Rory." They grabbed my arm.

I licked my lips. "They're... confused. I think. But cis people almost always are. They'll get used to it."

"You know I'm not then?" He checked. "Cis?"

I rolled my eyes. "You came out extremely publicly at the end of a school mandated performance. I'm not that bad at paying attention."

"I meant..."

"Are you cis?" I checked.

"Don't think so."

"Then cool. I know."

"It won't work like that though. For most people."

I sighed. I'd invited them over to practice, not for a pep talk. I was never good at those. "They'll get used to it. And if they don't, fuck them."

She shook her head. "I can't do that."

I knew that already. It's one of the only things I could confidently say I was better at then him. "Then it's a good thing this is an away tournament so you can practice telling people to fuck off without it mattering. As long as they're not judging our rounds," I added. "Pronouns?"

"I think I'm equally good with any."

I frowned at that. I definitely wasn't good with any and wasn't accustomed to nonbinary people who weren't me.

He sighed. "I can just go if you're gonna–"

"Fuck no, we're way behind already. Have you picked out a new name yet?"

"I don't think I'm going to. I like Finn, it's a solid name."

I was better at hiding my confusion at that. It would take me years to realize that she'd never said, "I don't like Finneas" and might not be correcting people because she actually didn't care at all, not because she didn't have enough of a spine to. Finneas was so far removed from anything anyone below the age of eighty would consider a solid name that I didn't even entertain it. By the time I'd realized, it felt too late both to ask or switch back.

"Cool. Let's get to work then."

Rory: Day 10 in the Bunker

Not even an apocalypse can stop Finn from being disgustingly chipper.

Despite usually being the one to get mad at me for using too many alarms during tournaments, they set one for seven the next morning and refuse to let me sleep past it. And then, they don't stop.

She draws up a schedule and refuses to let me add any form of input but makes it abundantly clear that I'll be expected to follow it nonetheless. I will, but I'm going to act as annoyed by it as I feel. You don't get to pull someone to the end of the world with you and then ignore his attempts at maintaining some form of normalcy. Normal Rory would also become a piece of shit the moment anyone tried to tell them what to do, so bitching about it is actually also me helping.

So, even though I spent hours playing and even longer complaining about playing, I let her win Monopoly. I have no particular want to obsess over a fake economy when the real one's probably gone forever and the faster we finish, the faster I can return to my bunk and pretend that none of this is actually happening. Besides, it seems like he could really use a win. Maybe it'll finally make them calm down.

As a thank you for boosting their ego, Finn throws a tiny metal boot at my face.

"What the fuck?" I jump to my feet, clutching my left eye. I can't tell if it made contact with the actual eyeball or just irritated the skin below it, but it still hurts like hell. Squinting through my good eye, I watch Finn clamour over the board to lean over me.

"Sorry," they say. "sorry, I–"

I push their shoulder. "What the fuck was that?"

"Sorry," he says again. "Let me–"

"Leave me alone!" I shove her again. Finally, she gets the hint.

I push myself to my feet and go find water to splash onto my face. I don't trust the cleanliness of a game piece that's been sitting down here for who knows how long.

When I return, Finn's already put the game away. I'm expecting him to apologize again. Apologizing is a very Finn move. Instead, she stands up, walks straight up to me, and says, "you let me win."

I've always hated it when they get close to me like that. I can practically feel their breath on the top of my head as they stare down. I don't like being reminded that anything about Finn Williams is bigger than me.

I don't back up. He's practically daring me to back up.

"You tried to blind me." I'm fine. When I finally forced my eye opened and checked it in the mirror it was a little red, but otherwise normal. It still hurts like a bitch though and it's not like I'm going to pass up the chance to throw that in her face.

She doesn't flinch. Instead, Finn Williams–nice, good, selfless, kind–says, "you cheated."

I roll my eyes. "Losing's not cheating."

He shakes his head. "It is though. Games only work if all parties involve agree to give it their best effort."

"It was taking hours, Finn."

"And now basically none of that matters because you decided to cheat! You're supposed to be competitive. You're annoyingly competitive. You're the last person I thought would ever–"

"Everyone's fucking dead!" I explode. "Everyone either of us has ever loved is probably fucking dead and you're yelling at me over a children's game!"

Her chest retracts. Her shoulder slump, just slightly. It's enough that it no longer feels like admitting defeat to walk past him.

"Rory." Finn grabs my arm.

I pull myself free, but they just grab on again.

"Rory, I shouldn't have–"

"I'm tired, okay?" I sigh. "I just want to sleep early and long. Just once. Let me fucking do that?"

"Sleeping all the time isn't good. We should try and–"

"I'm tired, Finn."

He lets go. "If you sleep past nine I'm waking you."

"I'll yell at you about it."

"Understood."

I crawl under the covers. I wait for them to yell at me about brushing my teeth because they've spent days micromanaging my entire routine, but they don't. Maybe I should get slightly injured more often. I curl up and let my aching eyes fall shut.

"It's seriously not good to start letting ourselves sleep just because we're bored, Rory," Finn says, because she can never get all the way to tolerable. "We have to keep finding things to–"

I wave an arm in what I'm pretty sure is her general direction.

"In the morning," I say.

What I don't say is that I'm not bored. What I don't say is that I have no idea how they could possibly be bored. I feel like every inch of my body has been wide awake for a week. I feel like that week's lasted months. I had always pegged Finn as the kind of person to either start bouncing off the walls in an emergency situation or to shut down completely but instead, she went manically productive. That was supposed to be my job. What I don't say is that I'm too exhausted for that to be my job.

I let my eyes stay closed, I couldn't get them to open now even if wanted to. I try to make my breathing regulate enough that they'll hopefully give up on me and go back to the storage room to find something else to occupy themself with. Then, when I'm sure she isn't looking anymore, I slip a hand further down the blanket, find my inner thigh, and run my fingertips against the red, raised, skin.

It's spread now. It was smaller than an egg yesterday and now it's bigger than my fist. Hopefully if I keep pretending it's not there, it'll go away on its own.

Rory: Day 11 in the Bunker

"Rory."

I'm tired enough that I make the mistake of pulling the blanket tighter against me the first time he says my name. Her own alarm hasn't even gone off yet though, so I squeeze my eyes shut and hope that they didn't notice me moving.

"Rory," they say again.

This time, I stay still.

And then, "Rory!"

I give up and roll over. "Holy shit, do you ever shut up?"

"I don't think so," Finn admits. She's turned the light on and is currently sitting cross-legged between our bunks, staring up at me.

I turn on my phone and sigh. "Finn."

"I'm sorry."

"It's 1am."

"I know. I'm sorry."

"You promised–"

"I know." They stand up. "Can I come up?"

I roll my eyes. "You're gonna do it anyway, right?"

She climbs up. Instead of explaining why I'm awake at 1am when she gets here though, Finn just swings their legs over the edge of the bunk, tapping their fingers together.

"What are–" it's all it takes for his attention to snap to me.

"I want to see your eye," she says.

"I... what?"

"To make sure it's okay. I didn't check."

"I'm fine," I tell them.

"I still need to see."

I sigh, leaning towards him. They lean back. I know that there's no sign of damage so when their eyes flit around my face,

I'm not sure what she's looking for. He nods once, apparently satisfied, and backs out of my personal space.

"I'm sorry I lost it. Earlier."

I roll my eyes. "You barely lost it."

"I hurt you."

"I've done worse."

"I yelled at you."

"I did that too."

She sighs. "I just... I don't want this to change me."

"What?" I ask. "End times?"

"Exactly." He is completely, absolutely serious because he's Finn, so of course he is. "I don't lash out at people over nothing."

"You used to," I remind them.

"I grew up."

"And I didn't?"

She leans back. The bed's way too small to accommodate anyone lying in that direction and her legs dangle so low that I'm convinced they'll pull her off the bed with them, but she stays still. "You're not... I don't think you do that. Over nothing."

I snort. "You're so full of shit." If Finn's decided not to be afraid of gravity, that means that I can't be either. I join them in staring at the ceiling. "See? Proof you're not changing. You still lie to avoid conflict whenever possible. Very on brand."

"I'm not doing that."

I roll my eyes. "I'm a dick, Finn."

"You're–"

"It's fine. I'm very aware. Dicks get things done. I'm going to–was going to–get things done."

"I think you're a probably secretly good person," they admit.

"Of course you do. That's your whole thing."

"You only lash out over things you care about. You're just too stubborn to admit that you care about things, so you pretend it's because you like pissing people off."

"I care about a lot of things," I protest. "I'm very open about that. I also like pissing people off."

"Only when they deserve it though."

"And you."

"Yeah, well," he rolls—even more precariously—onto his side. "I'm special."

I do the same. I'll never not meet a challenge from Finn Williams.

"I've decided," they say slowly. "I've decided that the asteroid was supposed to be huge, right? And they probably knew about it for who knows how long before the leak. So, they were ready, they just didn't want anyone to know because everyone would be travelling all over the place, but they have a ton of secret interconnected bunkers and late Friday night, they went door to door and ordered everyone into them."

I nod, mouth suddenly dry. "Okay."

"So they're all fine. They wanted to come get us, but they were under strict orders to evacuate everyone immediately and figured we'd be safe underground. But everyone else is fine. We're the only fucked ones."

"Okay," I repeat.

Finn rolls back over to stare at the ceiling. I let my chest loosen when his eyes aren't on mine. At least when she's not watching, I don't have to pretend to believe her.

"I bet my mum's losing her shit," they say. "when things calm down she'll probably order them to march right out here in like, hazmat suits or something and then never let me out of her sight for the rest of eternity. Fair warning, she'll probably murder you on sight. Once they come for us, make sure your underground tunnel areas never overlap with my underground tunnel areas."

"Got it."

"My sisters? They'll be pissed too. She's probably extra helicoptery right now. I'll just get a cool future job and buy them ice cream or something. They're still at the age where that fixes everything, you know? What about you?"

I swallow. "Finn, I can't—"

Her fist presses against my side. "Rory," he says. Her voice shakes as she repeats the question. "What about you?"

I lick my lips. "My dad was convinced that the leak couldn't possibly be real. I don't think my mom'll ever let him live that down. They're probably trying to figure out how to get themselves elected leaders of the mole people or something."

"Good." Finn nods. "Then they'll corral people to come get us in no time."

I know I won't be able to respond to that without my voice shaking, so I don't.

"My friends are gonna appreciate me so much more when they find out I'm not dead," Finn says. "Your girlfriend too. She'd probably—"

"Ex."

"What?"

"We broke up. Last summer."

"Oh," she says. "You seemed... I'm sorry."

I have thought about Alice far less than I should have. I've thought about everyone far less than I should have because as long as I don't think about them, they get to stay safely frozen in time. You don't get to drag someone to the end of the world with you and then put your coping mechanisms above theirs though, so I talk. "Don't be, I broke up with her. Plus, we're still friends so I'm sure she's still... you know. Missing me."

"They're going to feel so stupid, right?" His voice wavers. "They've probably mourned us already and everything. They're going to feel so dumb when they realize that they didn't have to."

"The dumbest," I whisper. There's no point concealing how tight my voice is anymore if they're also doing a shitty job at believing themself.

"And when we get back," Finn continues. "We never have to talk again. We probably shouldn't, honestly. Like I said, my mum's slightly murderous. But for now, we need... pretend to like me, okay?"

"That'd be wildly out of character." I say it because they're expecting me to. You don't get to drag someone to the end of the world with you then say no to the one thing they ask of you.

"I know, but I need... everyone else who likes me probably thinks I'm dead right now. I need someone to know I'm alive and believe that I'm good enough to be worth wanting me to that way."

I roll my eyes. "You're such a people pleaser."

"I know," he says again. "And I know you hate that about me so it's probably not helping, but—"

"Finn," I stop her. "I'm just being annoying. Obviously. You've spent forever pretending to tolerate me, I can obviously do that for a bit too."

They nod. "Thank you. We'll be out of here in a few weeks anyway so it's not like it'll matter at all pretty soon," they quickly add.

I just nod.

She switches positions to face me again. "I'm sorry I woke you to apologize," they whisper. "I know that probably didn't help I just..."

"It didn't."

Her face goes red. "Right, sorry, I—"

"Finn. Just being annoying. Again. I love it when people grovel for me."

They laugh. "You're going to make a really, really good power-hungry dick someday."

"Thanks," I nod. I'm supposed to smile but my breath catches in my throat. "I like to think so too."

Rory: Anytime Before Impact

I think sometimes people look to the fact that Finn's never deadnamed me and I've never misgendered her and use that as an excuse to say that we never really hated each other. I know people have thought that about him for a fact, anyway, as if you could treat somebody like shit for years then get their pronouns right and prove that you were secretly the bigger person all along.

We did hate each other though. We have for years. Supervillains don't have to randomly call the heroes by some other name to prove that they're evil because most people's names and genders aren't treated like privileges.

Finn is an asshole. He's an asshole capable of memorizing a four letter name, but that has nothing to do with whether or not she's an asshole. They always have been and always will be the absolute worst.

Rory: Day 11 in the Bunker

When I wake up again for real, it's with a cough and a headache.

These are both explainable phenomena. I've been drinking from a probably poorly installed filtration system and recently went through a massive diet change. I know that Finn will freak if she finds out though, so I triple check that they're not in the room before letting myself cough into my sleeve. I down an entire cup of water and when my throat feels semi-fine again, I go to find her.

Finn handles breakfast. And dinner. He occasionally lets me fend for myself at lunch, but she normally takes over that too. I'd feel guilty if it wasn't so incredibly convenient. I'm an awful cook and they keep insisting on it anyway, so I let them have it. He's sitting down at the tiny kitchen table reading when I get there, pots covered on the stove.

"Hey." When I speak, my voice is smooth and normal. I am fine.

When she lowers the book, her eyebrows are hidden beneath her bangs. "Holy shit, you're conscious."

I roll my eyes, walking past them to check out the stove. He's made oatmeal. We eat way too much oatmeal.

I scoop some into a bowl anyway. Heat'll be good for my throat.

"It's barely noon."

"I've been up all morning."

"Of course you have."

I plop down across from him and point my spoon at the book. "You'll run out of those at this rate, you know. Try being lazy and boring like the rest of us."

Finn shrugs. "I can just reread them."

"Of course you have the same taste as elderly conspiracy theorists."

Her face goes red. It's the most interesting thing that's happened for days.

"Oh my god," I lean forward. "What have you been reading?"

"This," they flap their book at me. "Is just *Little Women.*"

"Right, and what super weird shit did they shelve beside it?"

He sighs. "You have access to the storage room too, you know. You can just check."

"But then I don't get to watch you be all embarrassing."

Finn rolls her eyes. "You said you'd be nice."

"No, I said I'd act like I believe you are. This is like, the closest to nice I get anyway."

"Fine." I'm expecting him to go blushing and sheepish again but instead, they put their elbows on the table and lean forward. Finn stares into my very soul before saying "porn."

I bark out a laugh. "I mean, obviously. What else would men pack for—"

"Alien porn."

I stare back.

"Boxes and boxes of it. And shitty alien romance novels. They saved a whole shelf for it." Her tone's flat and her expression is completely neutral. She somehow thinks that she's turned this around on me.

I relax my own features and mimic their posture. "No wonder you've been reading so much recently."

"It's extremely academically stimulating."

"I'm sure. Do you think they're his or hers?"

"Hers. Lots of scantily clad women getting it on with multi-armed muscly alien men."

"Good for Madge."

"I know. Very progressive." The corner of their mouth ticks up, a tiny almost laugh escaping from the gap it forms.

I jump out of my chair and point in triumph. "That was a laugh!"

"Yeah," she says slowly. "because alien porn is objectively funny."

"That's not... you cracked first! I won!"

"I have no idea what you're talking about."

I lunge across the table to hit him, but she catches my fingers. "Careful. You'll spill your breakfast."

"You suck."

"You said you'd pretend you liked me."

"I know. You just make that incredibly hard."

Her expression falls. She releases my hand, pushes back against her chair, and gets up. "I'm gonna clean up and go take stock of all the things in the storage room," they mumble, heading towards the door.

I sigh. "Wait." Even saying it makes me wince. "You know I wasn't... I'm full of shit. You know that. I don't think... you're okay. Ish."

Finn grins. Way too quickly.

"Oh fuck y—"

"Look at you apologizing for hurting my feelings."

"I didn't apologize for anything," I point out. "For the record. I was just reminding you that I'm not a good person because you tricked me into believing that you were dumb enough to forget that. That says more about you than me."

"Not even a tournament in sight for you to blame being human on this time."

"I'm actually going to kill you one day."

"No you won't. You think I'm okay."

"I said ish!"

They shrug. "Sure. I'm gonna go take inventory for real now. Feel free to be useful for once and help."

"I know where you sleep!" I yell after her.

He raises a single middle finger over his shoulder and walks away.

Rory: Day 12 in the Bunker

When I wake up, it's to blackness.

I'm suspended in the air or underwater. It's not heavy or light, it just isn't. It's a blackness so thick that while I can feel my neck moving so I'm certain that I must still have a body, I can't see my own hand even when I hold it just in front of where my face should be.

I can feel eyes on me. Dozens of eyes. Hundreds. Thousands. They're staring and seeing, somehow, through all this darkness. I hear no voices, but the rustling of blinking eyelashes is deafening.

They must be close to be able to see me through all this black. I try to twist my body but the dark is too heavy—or maybe too light—for me to get any traction. They're staring—each and every one of them. They're wanting.

I open my mouth. I've always associated darkness with night and the cold, but it feels hot as it presses against my throat.

"Who are you?" I ask.

They don't respond, but it's not their fault. I can't even hear my own voice.

I try again, louder. "What do you want?"

The blackness blinks.

"What do you fucking want!"

I no longer care about the dark or the floating or the thousands of eyes. The worst part—the most terrifying part—is moving my mouth and feeling my own vocal cords vibrate and not hearing any of that produce a single sound. I'm drowning in the blurred line between thoughts and words.

"Leave me the fuck alone!" I not-yell. "I can't do anything for you! It's not my fault!"

The darkness is no more capable of hearing or speaking than I am, so the thousands of eyes just keep blinking. If I am all that's left, then there's nothing more for it to do than watch.

"Rory!"

My first instinct upon discovering that my limbs can move again is to push against every single muscle all at once.

Finn curses, grabbing at the edge of my bunk.

I reach half consciousness just in time to wrap an arm around their middle to help her stabilize herself.

He must have woken up and gone straight for my bed before the lights. I need both their brightness and buzz right now, but I'm not about to admit that. Instead, I listen to her breathe through the darkness and blink until my eyes adjust enough to vaguely make out her outline.

"You good?" She checks.

"I didn't mean to push you."

"I know. It's fine."

"You shouldn't just forcibly wake people up in the middle of the night. Especially on bunk beds. It's a safety hazard."

He sighs. My early morning act of heroism has placed us close enough to each other that I feel a short burst of warm air hit the top of my head. The reminder that both air and motion still exist slows my pounding heart.

"You were screaming," she says.

Shit. "Oh."

"I figured I should—"

"I didn't ask you to wake me."

"I know."

"I actually specifically remember saying that you should stop doing that."

"I know."

"If you wake me up again tomorrow, I'll make your life a living hell. There's nowhere to hide from me here either, so you know I'm good for it."

"Fine. Whatever."

I squeeze my eyes shut and let out a slow, measured breath. I'm still in motion too. "Thank you."

"Holy—"

"Make this a thing and I'll never say it again."

She laughs. "Wanna talk about it? Or... anything?"

"Definitely not." I roll my shoulders. Stretch out a kink in my neck. "Did you... did I say anything?"

"Nope. Just made a series of random screeching noises. Very hot and cool."

I groan. "This fucking sucks."

"It was just a nightmare. Most people—"

"You were supposed to be the one to have one first though."

They're quiet.

"Shit," I realize. "I didn't... I obvious don't like, want you to be scared."

"I am," she whispers. "Terrified."

"Me too," I admit. It'd be stupid to keep trying to hide it. "I'm just... I work well with logic? It's kind of my thing. Fear's one of the least logical emotions and I don't know how to... you're emotional."

He exhales. "Gee, thanks."

"Not in a bad way. Just... a different one, I guess? It's why you keep tricking people into liking you without even realizing that you're tricking them. I know how to deal with you freaking out. I don't know how to fix it when I am."

They're quiet again.

"Finn?" I hear my voice spike. I hate that that means that he also hears my voice spike. With no windows down here, it's sometimes hard to forget that other people still exist in the darkness. "Are you—"

Fingers grab my wrist. "Right here."

I know she's touching me because she heard the anxiety in my voice and that that means that I should pull away out of principle, but I'm not ready to be alone yet.

He's quiet for another moment, but I can feel him against me. I decide that that means that I'm still okay.

"Can I say something that'll kind of make me sound like an awful person?"

I sit up a little bit taller. "Well now you have to."

"I'm kind of glad," they admit. "That you... it's nice to know that you're scared."

"Wow," I deadpan. "You're a horrible person."

"Shut up!" Her hand comes off my wrist but then it's hitting my shoulder, so I'm still fine.

"I'm serious. Worst I've ever met."

"You suck."

I shrug. "At least I own it. Even I said I didn't want you to be scared. Ha. Nicer."

They sigh. Maybe they know that I'm itching to get up and turn on the lights now that their hand's gone again, because their head flops right onto my shoulder. "You've just... you seemed so calm, you know?"

"I do nothing all day unless you bully me into it. I seem lazy."

"Still though, you're calm lazy. I didn't... feeling like you're freaking out alone sucks."

I roll my eyes even though he can't see them. "You're infinitely better at apocalypses than me. You've been freakishly productive about the whole thing."

"Because you've been acting like everything's totally fine!"

"Because you are!" I sigh. "I promise to fall apart visibly at least once a week if you do. Until our parents overthrow the government and come rescue us or whatever."

They sit back up. "Good. Deal. I'll umm... let you sleep."

I grab their arm in a panic before remembering how embarrassing that is. "Turn on a light or something down there, okay? So you don't fall when you inevitably force me awake again in a few hours?"

"Got it."

I forget to let go of him, so Finn pulls my hand away, squeezes once, and disappears completely into the blackness.

Rory: Day 12 in the Bunker

Despite his promise to break down at least weekly, Finn's up at seven again the next morning. Their alarm wakes me too, but when she starts to say my name, I chuck a pillow at her and she gets the message, wandering into the kitchen on her own.

I wait until I hear the sink running to try and sit up.

I can feel my brain. It was a dull throb in the nighttime but now, it hits me at full force. It presses against my skull, trying to escape. I groan and ease myself into a seated position.

I could be dehydrated. I've probably been drinking less than normal. I just need to get up, drink some water, and I'll be fine.

Getting down the ladder takes way too long. I keep both hands tight on the rungs and move as slowly as I can, worried I'll lose my balance and cause a scene. I squeeze my eyes shut and collect my bearings once I'm firmly on the ground. This is nothing a few over the counter pills wouldn't fix and I'm sure any self-respecting doomsday preppers would've stocked up on tons of those, but knowing Finn, they've opened each box already to get an exact count of our supplies. I'll take something if this gets serious. For now, it's just a bit of dehydration.

I drink straight from the tap in the bathroom and splash water onto my face to try to shock my systems into functioning. For the first day in a while, I brush both my hair and teeth, wash my face, and put on the bit of mascara, foundation, and eyeliner I brought for the tournament. Looking good can psychologically make you feel good. I really hope that that still holds true when you're trapped underground with someone you're not trying to impress.

"You're awake," Finn calls from the cupboards when I drag myself into the kitchen.

I roll my eyes and sit down at the table. "Someone woke me."

"You want crackers and honey or crackers and peanut butter?"

I squeeze my eyes shut, taking a moment to shove my brain back into place. "You're allergic," I remember.

"Yeah, which is why you'd have to make it yourself. I'm not anaphylactic, as long as I don't physically eat it, we're all good."

"How about we don't risk any allergic reactions when it's literally impossible to get to emergency services?"

"Aww," they plop a box of crackers and jar of honey onto the table and sit down across from me. "you care."

"I just don't feel like sharing a room with a corpse. No opening allergens in an enclosed bunker."

"Got it." His eyebrows furrow. "You're wearing makeup."

I nod, getting to work preparing pathetic little fake sandwiches. "Brought it for the tournament. Figured looking awake would help me feel awake."

"Does it?"

I shake my head then instantly regret it, breathing through a wince. "I'm starting to think that that might only be true for people who regularly wear it. I've never really been a makeup person. I feel like I'm constantly aware of it whenever it's on my skin."

"I've never tried it."

"Definitely not worth it."

"Oh."

I finish an entire cracker sandwich before realizing. "Oh shit, was that... did you want to try mine?"

"It's fine."

"No, it's... I probably have tons. Like, all of it's incredibly boring and a lot of it's probably slightly expired since I normal just chuck stuff in my bag specifically for tournaments, but I'm sure it's still safe. I'm never going to use it all."

Finn bites into a cracker. I wince at the sound. This morning was definitely not a good time for crunchy foods. "This isn't another gender crisis," they say. "I'm not a girl."

"Cool. Neither am I."

I get up to escape her and her cracker crunches. "I'll go eat in the other room and dig through my bag. Come steal shit whenever."

There is way too much makeup in my bag.

I hide everything I used this morning in the side pocket right away—just because I don't want Finn knowing that I might be sick doesn't mean I'm planning on increasing his chances of catching it—and am still left with almost half a dozen of everything. Eyeliner pens and tubes of mascara, each shaped slightly different to achieve some purpose I was never able to figure out. Pallets of blush and eyeshadow that I never learned out how to use without looking slightly clownish. Even a few bottles of nail polish—red from when I'd read that that was a power move, black from when I'd decided that that actually was one, nude from when I'd thought that it would make me look more mature in ninth grade—that I can't believe hadn't shattered already.

I shouldn't have admitted that I didn't like makeup because then, at least, I'd have an excuse for why there's so much makeup in my bag that isn't just me confessing to being a massive hypocrite. Eye shadow feels like a stupid thing to hide in the middle of end times though, so I leave it all out between our bunks.

Finn gives up on asking for help at my third "does it look like I fucking know?" so I lean back, snack on crackers, and watch her try things out. It can be incredibly boring being trapped in a bunker with someone. Eventually, it gets bad enough to coax me into conversation.

"You've really never done this shit before?"

They grit their teeth, trying not to mess up the eyeliner they're attempting to apply. I'm nowhere near preceptive enough with makeup to know if he's actually doing a good job. "Nope."

"Huh. Figured you would've."

They turn so quickly that I'm surprised it doesn't leave a line of black on her cheek. "What the fuck does that mean?"

I blink. I know all the best ways to get under Finn Williams' skin without veering too close to actual anger, and this isn't supposed to even be on the map. This is why I don't do small talk.

"Geez," I put up my arms. "Forget it, okay? Whatever."

"I'm not a girl," they repeat.

I roll my eyes. "Yes, Finn, I know. Literally nobody ever has made that mistake."

"And what does that mean?"

I sigh. "You escalate things a lot. For someone who wanted us to pretend to be friendly."

"Because you keep saying stupid shit!"

"That was basically the most innocuous question I could have possibly asked."

They lean forward to grab one of my cracker sandwiches and I panic and slap their hand away. Which definitely isn't helping deescalate things.

She raises her eyes to mine. Only one of hers has eyeliner around it.

"I made these," I say, chest tight. "Get your own."

"I was only going to take one."

"Then go take one from the kitchen," I shrug. I move the plate onto my bed and out of their reach, just in case.

Finn stares. "You're not letting me take one cracker."

"They're mine."

"Even though I've been making you food. For days."

"I didn't ask you to do that."

"You... who the fuck are you performing for? We haven't seen anyone else for weeks—"

"Twelve days," I correct on impulse. Based on the glare that he shoots my way, that doesn't help.

"For weeks," Finn repeats. "And you still can't stop acting like a self-centred dick for more than two seconds at a time!"

I almost tell him then. About the rash and the coughing, the dizziness and the vomiting. I would risk my own destruction, just to prove Finn Williams wrong one last time. But hiding a potentially contagious mystery illness could definitely also be framed as selfish, so I bite my tongue.

She sighs, dropping her voice again and getting up.

My pulse spikes. "you're only half–"

"I know. I guess I'll have to take a break and go get my own snacks."

I don't do apologies unless they benefit me, and this one won't. I haven't done anything wrong. I asked an innocent question and protected someone from potentially fatal cross contamination. I've been doing everything right so if anything, Finn should apologize to me.

When they return, they pick the eyeliner back up, put their phone on the bed to use it as a mirror, and turn away from me. I almost laugh at how anti-climactic of a power move it is, but catch myself just in time. Since he's ignoring me, I do the same. I should have downloaded more games onto my phone. Without Wi-Fi, all I have is a lame jumping game that I've already unlocked everything in, but I play it anyway just to look busy. Finn's decided to be quiet and petty which is supposed to be my thing, so I guess we'll just be mutually petty until she goes back to normal.

Except, the boredom. The fourth time I watch him wipe botched nail polish off of the same nail, I cave.

"Give me your hand."

They don't respond.

"Finn. You're going to use up all the toilet paper."

"We have tons," she mumbles.

"Well then you're going to finish driving me insane. Give me your hand."

He doesn't.

I sigh, opening the black nail polish and doing my left hand. By the time I'm done, she's still on the same finger.

"Eh." I kick their side. "My left hand's too shaky. You'll have to paint my right."

They continue ignoring me. They're better at it than I thought they'd be.

"Finn. Finish my fucking nails or I'm confiscating all of my stuff."

She sighs, finally turning around. It's to glare at me, but it's still progress.

I smile a bit, holding out the brush. "I'm self-centred, remember? Make me all pretty."

He's still silent and bitter as he paints them, but at least he's another bitter, breathing, living person.

"Your turn." I hold out my hands when she's finished.

"Rory."

"Nope," I shake my head. "This is a transactional exchange. Hand and polish please."

She sighs, but relents. Finn's apparently a nail polish perfectionist, so I bite me tongue and work painfully slowly.

"This was a very me move," she remarks once I've finished the third finger.

I glance up.

"The nail polish thing. Feels like something I'd normally have to trick you into."

I shrug. "Guess I have a lot of experience with petty self-centred assholes." I get back to work. "Don't make me do it again. Being you's boring. Everything's supposed to revolve around me all the time and it can't do that if we both keep blowing up over nothing constantly."

"It's... things all just feel bigger. With... recent events."

"I know." What I really want to say is that things are obviously bigger for me too, but I can't let myself. Being Finn Williams must be exhausting.

"And I think I've always been more... sensitive? To gender stuff around you? Even before all of this."

"I'm extremely aware." I also don't take the opportunity to point out that that's bullshit because I've always given way more of a damn about getting their gender right than the people she actually likes. I haven't been perfect about it, but at least I've always actually cared.

His hand jerks. Luckily, I don't have the brush against her nail when it happens.

"You have to—" I start. But her fingers aren't in my hand anymore. I should have remembered that Finn's incapable of talking without their full range of motion at their disposure.

"You know I'm nonbinary, right?"

I frown. "What? Yeah. Hence the—"

"And I'm not less nonbinary than you just because I use more pronouns or less people acknowledge it or I'm not all the way out or—"

"You're not all the way out?"

"I'm not a cis guy with extra steps or a trans girl who's just not ready to commit to it yet just because I'm not nonbinary in the same way you are. You're not better at it than me, or whatever. You know that I'm not less nonbinary than you are just because I'm more subtle about it, right?"

I blink, trying to decide how Finn Williams would respond.

The real Finn sighs. "Forget it. This—"

"I'm better than everyone at everything," I go with. Filtering everything through someone else's brain takes too much time.

She rolls her eyes. "You're so—"

"You can't be better at gender though, so I guess yeah. I know."

He nods once. Places his hand back in mine. "You can keep—"

"Where did I fuck up?"

"It's nothing."

"No. I'll be trapped alone with you for who knows how much longer, Finn. You don't get to get mad at me for something then not tell me how I fucked up because I promise, I'll definitely find a way to do it again."

She sighs. "You didn't do anything. Technically."

"Okay," I lean back against my bunk. I have a feeling we won't be getting back to nails for a while. "What did I do generally then?"

They pick at their nailbed.

"Don't do that," I instruct. "You'll smudge the nail. It's easier to fix once it's dried."

He stops, but immediately starts picking at his dried hand.

A list of more accurate words to describe Finn Williams than 'nice': bouncy, loud, claustrophobic, in motion.

"I don't have to wear makeup," she says. "Or skirts or dresses or whatever just to prove that I'm queer."

"Good idea. Stereotypically masculine fashion's normally wildly more practical."

She doesn't respond.

"This was your idea," I remind him. "Or... technically I guess I mentioned it first, but only because you very heavily implied that you wanted to try stuff out."

"I know."

"You don't get to get pissed at me just because you decided to try something then realized that you didn't like it."

"I do," they say. "Or... I think I do."

I wait, but he's back to silent.

I sigh. "Still not really getting what you've decided I did wrong here, Finn."

"You never wear makeup," he says.

"Correct."

"Like, so rarely that it was instantly noticeable when you put on mascara."

"Yup."

"So why the fuck did you think it was weird that I'm not a makeup person when you're not either?"

I roll my eyes. "I said it was weird you've never tried it before, Finn. I have. Like 90% of your friend group is girls who like makeup and I just figured girls who like makeup wouldn't let you go that long without trying makeup?"

She just says, "oh." Then "sorry."

Something swells in my chest. "Holy shit," I realize. "Is this how you feel whenever I have to apologize for freaking out about nothing? We should do this more often."

"You actually very rarely apologize for that," he points out.

"Maybe you should try harder to get me to, then. This rocks."

They roll their eyes. "They have tried," he admits. "My friends."

"Oh my god you weren't only wrong, I was also right?"

"You were still a dick about snacks," they remind me.

I shrug. "I've always been a dick about snacks. Didn't want to shock your system." I pop another cracker into my mouth to accent the point. "So, why not get your much more makeup savvy friends to lend you stuff instead of me?"

"I think they think I'm gay?"

I frown, confused.

"I mean I am," he says. "Gay. But in the other direction. I feel like I'm pretty open about being a lesbian but every time they offer it feels very gay-best-friend patronize-y? I don't really know how to describe it. Or like they've convinced themselves that I'm just a secret trans girl waiting to come out of her shell? Which I know doesn't make sense because not only girls and gay guys wear makeup and I genuinely did want to try it out, I just... wanted to try it out because my gender doesn't matter instead of as a sign of how much it does? Which I know's—"

"I broke up with my girlfriend because she was being too nice to me," I interrupt. When you let Finn get talking for too long, they never stop. While that'd normally be a good thing while trying to fight off the loneliness of everyone else I've ever known probably being dead, I'm half that convinced she'll talk until the sun itself explodes if I let her.

He frowns. "You... what?"

"Alice is great. And straight which like, shouldn't have been an issue because nonbinary people are supposed to fit into pretty much any dating label and I'd known her for years before we started dating and she never once made it seem like she thought I wasn't nonbinary? But then we started going out and she suddenly started randomly telling me how handsome or strong or—"

Finn laughs at the strong part. They have the decency to blush when they notice me noticing.

"See? Things that were obviously bullshit. And it just felt... weird? Like she knew I was nonbinary when we were friends but the moment we started dating she thought she had to coddle me and treat me way more masculinely than she literally ever had before. So, I broke up with her."

"Did you tell her you didn't like her saying stuff like that?"

I roll my eyes. "You've met me, what do you think? I was gonna slowly start casually complaining about other people doing stuff like that until she got the hint and then we'd start dating again once we'd fixed it. Easy." I swallow, mouth suddenly dry. I don't know how I could have possible started casually talking about her. I'm not supposed to be letting myself think about any of them. "Which I guess was a waste of time now but—"

Finn draws a sharp breath.

I sigh, but it's quiet enough that I'm counting on him not noticing. "Nothing like a giant asteroid to destroy gender norms, right? I bet by the time I see her again most words won't even have gendered connotations anymore."

She nods, satisfied with my flimsy attempt to uphold her fantasy.

"I don't even hate the word handsome, just that she was only using it all of the sudden, I guess? The whole reason I'm nonbinary is because I'm neither gender. It still feels gross when people decide that the nicest thing they could possibly do for you is treat you like the opposite end of the binary from where you were assigned."

He nods again. "Like someone making a point of using every major pronoun except your assigned one."

I chew at my lip. "I stopped doing that. And that had nothing to do with your assigned gender, it was just an ill-advised attempt to balance things out. I've seriously never once thought you were a girl or demi-girl or whatever."

"Okay," he tells the floor.

"Plus most people only use one for you. And you said any was fine, not all, so I figured—"

"Any is. It just... you were the only other nonbinary person I knew when I first came out? It felt kind of shitty that instead of just choosing one or two or all of them, you made a big deal about specifically not using one? It's fine. I'm over it now." They're still not looking at me, so that's obviously a lie.

I sigh. "You're right, that sucked. I'm... sorry."

Finn's head snaps up, massive grin on display.

"No!" I realize. I have to stop letting myself forget that she's an actor. "You don't get to keep doing that!"

He laughs. "You're right. Getting other people to apologize does feel good."

I glare, unscrewing the nail polish again and holding out a hand. I bite back a grin when she puts her on top of mine. Mid-nails was a really risky time for a power play.

Rory: 10 Years Before Impact

I started a club in elementary school called the "Anti-Finneas Williams" club. It was during a particularly vicious streak of her being annoying. They'd shout out something stupid abruptly in class just to get us all held in for recess. Scribbled all over other people's free-draw work and pinched the forearm of any girl who got too close to them. It made recruitment exceptionally easy.

We didn't actually do much. Just made a few posters and spent a recess chanting and hunting her down—not to attack her, obviously. Just for more chanting. It got shut down within a day and I had to stay in the next recess for a lecture on "bullying" even though the amount of supporters I'd managed to amass obviously proved that if anything, Finn was running a bullying empire. It was my first taste of what I considered to be grave injustice, but I didn't know how to argue for myself yet, so I sat in all break and sulked.

Rory: Day 14 in the Bunker

While I had never considered what I would do in an apocalypse until it was too late, I think my life was always going to revolve at least a bit around Finn Williams. We've been on a collision course since we were four. She was a menace then my nemesis then somehow, all at once, the person that all of our teachers wished that I could be. My greatest competition and asset.

Alice was wrong to be jealous of Finn. I have never had romantic feelings for Finn. But her worries were not complete unfounded. I think it'd be impossible to not become at least a little obsessed with somebody that the universe keeps slamming you into.

I'd never considered apocalypses before, but now, it makes a weird sort of sense that even in my most isolated state—even when I might be all that's left in the world—she's here too. The universe would never let me off the hook over something as inconsequential as a mass extinction event.

We adjust to our end too quickly but then, there's nothing to fight against. We get good at cohabiting and polite niceties. If we avoid talking about anything of consequence, Finn's almost an enjoyable person to be around.

The problem though—what they don't get and maybe never will—is that I need consequence. If the world is ending and I can't fight that, I need to fight something. I cannot pull someone to the edge of the earth with me then ask them to let me yell at them for a bit though, so I learn to bite my tongue.

Finn and I have been on a collision course since four, so she notices. In the middle of our tenth game of checker of the day, they push the board away.

"This house supports the use of uniforms in schools."

I frown. "What?" It's an intro motion. Boring and easy to argue from either side. So basic that they'd used it at two initial recruitment meetings during my time on the team.

"Let's run it. Right now."

I roll my eyes. "That's a lame motion."

"Figured I'd have to ease you into it. This is probably the longest you've gone without imagining all they ways you'd destroy nonexistent people's arguments as you fall asleep."

"I don't do that!" I have definitely done that. It's important to imagine yourself arguing against every hypothetical opposition.

Finn pulls out their phone. "I'll set a timer. We'll both just go twice since we don't have partners. If you think you'd have enough material to cover that long, that is."

"Fuck you."

"You taking prop or opp?"

"You can choose. You're the one who needs the advantage."

He laughs. "We'll flip for it."

I pull my bag over to grab my loonie. I don't ask who's who. We never have to. I watch it flip and check to confirm that it's landed on tails.

"Your pick."

"Opp."

I didn't have to ask about that either. That's the side with the gender inclusivity argument and Finn always, always, goes for that one. I know that. I know him. It's why I'm going to completely destroy them.

"Ready?" She checks.

I smile. I've never been more ready for anything.

We spend two hours arguing about things that no longer matter. There's no one to judge and Finn does an admirable job, but I decide that I've won each and every round.

Then, his obnoxious alarm goes off and I do my best to conceal a wince. I'm adjusting to the molten lava splashing around in my brain, but the alarms never get easier.

Finn stops mid-speech, says "dinner time," and disappears. It's sacrilegious.

But it's not, to them. They've never cared about debate the right way. She likes it because she likes having an audience to perform to, not as an exercise in logic and reasoning. And here, there's no audience.

Apocalypses are supposed to bring out the worst in people. Disaster is when "good" people—the ones everyone's always raving about—show their dark undersides. Finn Williams greets the apocalypse with schedules, optimism, and feigned investment in other people's coping mechanisms.

A list of more accurate words to describe Finn Williams than 'nice': bouncy, loud, claustrophobic, in motion, nice. Ish.

Rory: Day 15 in the Bunker

"Can we talk?"

Finn's always obscenely energetic, no matter the hour. I've come to count on it. Being trapped with one of the most alive people in existence makes it easier to forget that everyone else you know might not be anymore. Opening a bathroom door expecting to have a few more minutes to prepare myself enough to feign at functioning and finding her bouncing right outside it is far from comforting though.

"Don't we always?"

I move past them to the kitchen. I was planning on sitting down and watching them make breakfast. At least I'll be able to follow through on the sitting part.

He sits down across from me. "I need to tell you something. But you can't freak out, okay? Neither of us can afford to freak out right now."

"Yeah, obviously."

He stares right at me. "Promise me."

"What?"

"Swear you won't freak out."

I roll my eyes and put a hand to my heart. "I solemnly—"

"Rory! I'm serious."

"You can't ask me to promise when I don't know what I'm promising to. If it's something freak out worthy, I might freak out a bit." For a moment—a ludicrous moment probably brought about by the dizziness—I think they're about to say that this has all been an elaborate scheme. Some weird attempt at team bonding.

Finn sighs. Her leg bounces so rapidly that the whole table shakes. "Just... promise you won't hate me then, okay?"

"Okay," I say it too quickly for someone who's supposed to hate everything about them. Too certainly for someone who's been pretending that they still do.

He shuts his eyes and takes another breath.

"Finn," I reach across the table to cover her hand with mine. "It'll be fine." It feels like the kind of lie they'd tell, so it seems like the best way to coax answers out of them.

"It's not," she shakes her head, eyes going glossy. "It won't be. It—"

"Finn." I repeat. "I can't help you figure it out unless I know what's going on."

They take one last giant breath. "I think I might be sick."

My world tilts on its axis.

"It's... I've been nauseous and lightheaded and I was hoping I was just hungry but it's been over twenty four hours and it won't go away?"

I swallow. "Finn."

"And I have a few of these little rashes that seem like they're spreading? I swear I thought it was just because of the change in soap brands and stuff. I would have mentioned them instantly if—"

"Finn."

"I thought it was anything serious. I think it's too late to isolate if it is though? It'd probably have to be airborne, so you've already been exposed and I really, really—"

"Jesus Christ, Finn! I've been sick for almost a week!"

They freeze. "Oh." I don't know if the sound of her chair scraping against the floor is actually deafening, or if it's just because of my head. "I umm... guess it doesn't really matter then. I'll boil water for breakfast."

I get up to follow him. "You can get mad."

"I'm not." She passive aggressively fills a pot.

"I would be. You... I get I should have said something right away. You did. You're allowed to be pissed about that."

"I'm not," they lie again.

"I'm sorry." I grab his arm to try and make him face me. "I was just scared that you'd—"

She spins around so suddenly that I lose my grip. "I didn't lock you out."

"I'm—I know."

"I heard you coughing and wheezing and obviously I knew that that meant that there was a really good chance that you'd been in contact with something dangerous and I still didn't lock you out. I didn't even fucking consider it."

"I know."

"You thought I'd what? Barricade myself away with all the food just because you were sick with something I'd already been exposed to? What the fuck, Rory?"

"I didn't..." I lick my lips. "Of course not. I never thought you'd... you wouldn't."

It's supposed to be reassuring, but instead, her eyes go wide. Her expression darkens. "You would've though, right?"

"I'm—"

"No! If I'd just told you that and you didn't already know that you were also sick, what would you have done?"

I'm supposed to lie. I'm supposed to keep my eyes on theirs and lie better than I have my entire life. But her eyes are too intense and my brain's too loud to think straight and for a second—less than one—my eyes dart towards the storage room.

"Holy shit, Rory!"

"I'm sorry." I'm not even sure they hear it. My voice is suddenly thick and hoarse.

"You'd let me starve to death just so—"

"You wouldn't. There's stuff in the cupboards and my bag's on your side. I still have a few things in there."

He glares, not appreciating the correction. "You'd let me die alone just to what? Buy yourself a bit longer of staying trapped here all by yourself until you follow suit?"

"You're the one who keeps saying they'll come for us!" I point out. "It'd make sense to try and last longer in case—"

"We both know that that's bullshit!"

I stare. They stare back. I'm shaking or they are or maybe we both are.

"I'm sorry," I say again, hopefully more audibly this time. "I'm not... I'm not a good person. I've never tried to lie about that."

"You're seriously fucked up, Rory."

"I'm sorry," I say again.

He sighs, putting an arm on my shoulder. For a moment, I flinch. Not because I think she'll hit me, but because I know I that would. They're right. I was afraid of them finding out because my biggest fear is Finn responding to things the way that I know that I would. She's not me though, so she just pushes me out of her way and abandons her pot in the sink.

"I need space. You can handle breakfast for once."

"Finn, I–"

She holds up a hand to stop me, not even bothering to turn around. "I don't ask you for a lot, all things considered. I just want some fucking space. Leave me alone, Rory."

"Okay," I whisper. "I can do that."

I put the pot on the stove then go rummage through storage until I find Advil. I open the door to the main room a crack to slip Finn the box alongside a bowl of oatmeal, but other than that, I spend the rest of the day completely alone.

Rory: 6 Years Before Impact

On the last day of school when I was twelve, we did this massive team scavenger hunt all over the neighborhood. We were in the lead. Until I twisted my ankle and tore up my knees on the pavement on the way back.

Finn was the only person who stayed with me. I kept telling them to go—yelling, really. He was definitely not the person I wanted nearby while I tried to fight off tears—but she refused. She helped me back until we reached the nearest teacher and when they invented a special "team player" award, I decided that that was why he'd done it. To show off. To trick people into thinking that they were selfless. To spite me.

But maybe, they'd just known that I'd needed help.

Rory: Day 16 in the Bunker

Finn spends the day in the main room, so I spend all day avoiding it. Beyond slipping in to use the bathroom once when I physically can't wait any longer, I never go past the kitchen door. I wait until I hear the lights go out to sneak into the bathroom again in the night and luckily, sleeping on a cool tile floor means that I wake frequently enough to use it again before they wake up.

I'm doing my best to prove myself capable of putting other people's needs and boundaries before my own, so when I lie down again to try and get a bit more sleep only to be woken up by her glaring down at me, I'm confused.

"What the fuck, Rory?"

I blink away grogginess and push myself up onto my palms. "What?"

"I literally just said I'd never lock you out! I wouldn't let someone fucking starve just because I'm pissed!"

I frown. "I know, I wasn't–"

"Stop treating me like I'm you!"

I blink. Pre-apocalypse Rory would resent that. They'd scream right back and shove it in her face that they were actually just doing exactly what she had asked them too. Post-apocalypse Rory wants to too. Every Rory has always hated change and not screaming back feels like too big of one. They've been waiting for something to lash out at.

But Finn is not my something. I'm supposed to be theirs.

"You're right," I say. "I'm sorry."

She sighs, pinching her brow. "You feeling okay today?" they ask, because they're Finn.

I am. I've gotten the volume in my brain down low enough to hear myself think again which honestly, might be worse. I nod. "I am. Are you–"

"I'm fine." He walks to the cupboard.

“I’m umm…” I try. “I’m already awake at an ungodly hour so if you wanted to do your whole–”

The cupboard slams shut. They walk back towards the bedroom, armed with honey and crackers. “I’ll leave your backpack by the door. Your phone’s probably getting low.”

It’s not. Last night was too quiet so I’d already tip-toed in to grab my headphones and charger. Handing over my backpack means two more seconds of potential human contact though, so I just nod.

“I’m sorry,” I try one last time.

They go.

Rory: Day 17 in the Bunker

I wake to the sound of the door slamming shut.

I've been sleeping with the lights on for almost a week so when the sound makes me bolt up on my mattress, I instantly see what's caused it.

"Finn?"

Even half asleep, it's obvious that something's wrong. Their eyes are wide and frozen. Her face is redder than I've ever seen it. They're breathing so quickly that I can hear it.

I jump to my feet. "What's happening? Are you... do you need a drink? I can get you a drink."

I turn towards the sink, but he grabs onto my arm. His actions are slow and staggering. I look her over.

"Hurt, scared, or both?"

I think I might hear the beginnings of a response, but they're wheezing too severely for anything to be coherent. For a moment, that sends me into a panic. Finn has an allergy. Not an anaphylactic one, apparently, but I know that they have at least one allergy. But I've seen everything he's taken from the kitchen recently, and none of it was new. I take a deep breath. Remind myself that panic, almost always, is ill-founded.

"Okay," I say. Their grip on my arm is getting sharp, so I carefully pry her fingers off, keeping them enclosed in one hand. I gently put the other against Finn's shoulder, guiding her down to the mattress. "You're okay, alright? I think you're just freaking out? I don't know over what so I can't fix that right now, but we'll deal with it." I sit down across from him and place my palms face up on my knees.

"Hands please."

They don't move.

"Finn. Hands."

I'm worried I'll have to grab them myself, but self preservation must win out, because she places hers on top of mine. "In through the nose on up, out through the mouth on down, right? Remember?"

Nothing. They're looking everywhere but me. That's not a good sign. "Finn." I nudge his knee with mine. "Remember?"

She only nods once, but it's enough.

I narrate the first few "in"s and "out"s aloud in case he wasn't actually paying attention then fall into mimicking their breathing.

"I don't..." he says, still mid-hyperventilation so I keep moving our arms. "I didn't want... your help."

I roll my eyes. "You're allowed to be pissed at someone and still use them for your own benefit. I do it all the time."

"I don't–"

"Finn." I stop her. "Less talking more breathing. I'm helping hostilely. That doesn't even count."

The moment they have their breathing back under control, he pulls his hands away. I get up to grab her a glass of water.

"I'm fine," they say. "I can–"

"Stay."

"I'm–"

"Holy shit, Finn. Let me do this one thing then you can go back to ignoring me forever, yeah?"

They stay seated.

"Here." I hand them the water, sitting back down to go through my bag. "You're not hurt, right? This was just... something else?"

He nods.

"Okay, good." I find what I'm looking for and open the tiny baggy of Sour Patch Kids. I hand her a yellow one. "Eat."

They shove my hand away. "I don't want pity candy."

"It's not pity candy, it's a tool. Chewing and sour flavours are both good for grounding. Take it."

She turns away.

"Take the fucking candy or I'm attacking you again. I'm not risking another panic attack just because you decided to be stubborn."

She sighs, but relents. She accepts the rest of the bag while slowly chewing on the yellow one.

"I'm not going to thank you," they say after a long moment. "I didn't ask for help."

"Good. You shouldn't."

I watch him eat another candy.

"What made you..." I start. "Are you okay?"

"I've been stuck underground with you for over half a month."

I wince. "Right, obviously. But something... did something make you less okay just now?"

He's quiet again. I almost convince myself that they're not going to tell me. But she's Finn, so of course she does. "If I'd tried that door later," he says slowly. "closer to the morning, would it have opened?"

"What? Of course."

She chews at her cheek. "You took your mattress. I woke up and your mattress—"

"You said you wanted space! I just didn't want to sleep on the floor every night."

He just keeps chewing. I resist the urge to tell her to eat another gummy instead. We don't have enough resources to treat infections.

"If we're both sick," I try to rationalize. "There'd be literally no reason—"

"You'd have all the resources though. And medication and—fuck! I can't even say that! I can't even say why I'm worried about it because I don't want to give you any fucking ideas!"

"There's more than enough for both of us," I point out.

"For how long? And we're arguing, so maybe you thought that it'd be more convenient to just freeze me out entirely!"

I sigh. "You shouldn't trust me. Not even just because I've given you a lot of reasons not to, you just... you really shouldn't trust me. It's good that you don't because I think I'm always going to put myself first. But I wouldn't... I don't want to die alone, Finn. I'm terrified... I could barely last two days of just feeling alone. Unless one of us becomes wildly infectious with something new and fast acting I wouldn't... I won't."

"I can't trust you."

"I know."

"No!" They exclaim. "I should be able to—you're the only person I can interact with! You're probably the last person I'm ever going to interact with and I can't fucking trust you to not just leave me for dead!"

"I know. I'm sorry." I think for a moment. "There are tools in the storage room, right? We'll figure out how to disable the locks. Or... we'll go through everything tomorrow and split it up so cutting access to one part of the bunker won't fuck anyone over. We'll figure it out."

"We need to do it right now."

I sigh. "What time is it?"

They click the side of their phone. "Two."

"We'll do it in the morning."

"But—"

"I'm sick, Finn. You are too. I know I've been feeling like shit basically constantly for days and there's no way that means that you're feeling fine even if it's progressing more slowly for you. We need to sleep."

She shakes her head. "I won't be able to. It's not fair that—"

"I know. You take the kitchen, I'll take the bedroom."

His attention moves to the door to the storage room.

I sigh. "You take the kitchen, I take the bedroom, then you lock the door behind me so I can't sneak past you and barricade myself into the storage room, okay? Which would be an idiotic move anyway since there's no running water there."

"There's lots of bottles, though."

"Okay. Lock the door then."

They hesitate. "I'll unlock it. In the morning."

"I know."

It's worse that I do. That she's so worried that I'd lock her out that she gave herself a panic attack over it, but I get to be so confident that he wouldn't that I'm the one to suggest locking it. I need to fix that. I don't know if I'm going to be able to fix that.

I do up my bag and throw it over my shoulder. "Night. Let me know if you need anything, okay?"

"Night."

I took the mattress from the bottom bunk, so I climb back up to the top. It's a good thing I did. It's only been a few weeks but when everything changes all at once, you cling onto the things that feel the same. I have never been a fan of change. I have never been a fan of change of any kind, but I know I'll have to, somehow. It wouldn't be fair to her if I didn't. I curl up against the wall, close my eyes, and try to will myself to fall asleep.

I don't know how many people are left in the universe. Hopefully, somehow, it's billions. Probably, it's closer to two.

And if it is—if the only two people left in all of existence are me and Finn Williams—then I am officially the worst person alive.

Rory: 3 Years Before Impact

At our second away tournaments, we stopped for food after. It was most people's favourite part of away tournaments. It was not mine. I had enough trouble socializing with my teammates even when you didn't have to factor in hearing them over the sounds of an entire restaurant.

We got fast food at least, which was slightly less awful. At least it would be over with quickly.

I sat as far away from Finn as possible. We always spent too much time together at tournaments and I think we both knew that if we pushed that much further, we'd kill each other. We'd all already started eating when I heard the waiter talking to the next table over about allergies.

It would have made the most sense to just say something at our table, but I panicked and pulled Finn around the corner to stand near the washrooms with me. He stared.

"You good?"

"They use peanut oil." I informed her. "For the fries?"

They smirked. "Yes, Rory, I'm actually capable of answering for myself when people ask about allergies."

"Cross-contamination could–"

"I'm fine. Promise I know more about how my body works than you do."

I nodded, face going hot. "Right then. Umm..."

"That was it? You kidnapped me just to talk about peanuts?"

"I didn't know if it was private."

They laughed. "Is someone else on the team planning a hit on me? Pretty sure–"

"You're so annoying!" I exclaimed. "I was trying to be helpful. Just..." I sighed. "Be careful, yeah?"

"Noted. Thanks for caring."

I was either going to hit her or myself.

"I just don't know if they'll let me change partners in the middle of the tournament. This isn't... you can die. Just after."

They laughed. "I'll keep that in mind."

Rory: Day 18 in the Bunker

When I report to the kitchen at 7am, the door's already unlocked. I'm not sure when Finn opened it and I'm not confident enough to ask.

"Are we eating first or sorting first?"

She sighs, still smoothing down her curls. I've caught her right after waking up. "I was overreacting last night. We don't actually have to divide everything up."

"We should. Important stuff, at least."

"I was overreacting," he repeats.

I choose my words carefully. "I'm not going to sudden steal everything so you technically were, but knowing you're overreacting doesn't exactly help when you're in the middle of freaking out. We should still divide things up."

Finn sighs again. "We can't keep isolating anyway. It's not healthy."

I don't let my relief show. I've already pressured Finn into the end of the world, I can't also guilt her into spending it with me.

"Okay," I say. "If you're sure."

"I'm still not... I'm not happy. With you."

"You shouldn't be," I nod. "And we should also still divide up essentials. Pills and food staples and stuff, just for reassurance."

"If we go back to living together it won't matter where we put stuff."

I consider. "You still have your bag, right? We'll put things in there and both carry ours everywhere we go."

They nod. "Okay. Sure."

"Everywhere," I reiterate. The moment I suggested it I knew that I wouldn't let my bag out of my sight, but Finn's good and expects the rest of the world to be too.

"Yeah, whatever."

"Finn." I look right at them. "Promise me you'll never let yourself get caught in a room without it, okay? Or even... even if you're also in the room, maybe don't leave it too close to me."

She frowns.

"I'm not going to do anything. I wouldn't be telling you to safeguard against it if I was genuinely planning on doing anything. I just..." I sigh. "Don't give me the option, okay?"

"Alright," he nods. "Whatever. Promise."

We split pills first. They're the smallest and easiest to fit. Advil and Tylenol and Gravol—everything over the counter that they've got. Then we do bandages and ointment. The only thing we leave behind is a single *Anti-Apocalypse* box that must have fallen behind the shelves before Madge could confiscate it because, for obvious reasons, neither of us have any intentions of taking those.

I don't point out that everything we find is meant to decrease symptoms, not cure them. I pop anything I safely can as soon as I safely can and keep the rest at the bottom of the bag. I pause between sorting out smaller food items and toiletries for the occasional sit-down or coughing fit.

I'm already trying to figure out how to get some of Finn's Advil. I try not to look. I try to distract myself with literally anything else as she slides them into the side pocket of their bag. If one of us deserves to survive an apocalypse, it's probably Finn.

I'll hate myself forever for doing it, but I'm already trying to figure out how to get the bag away from them. It's exactly why we have to be doing this.

We finish packing and return to the main room though once we get there, it's clear that neither of us knows how to proceed. Finn starts another puzzle. She doesn't tell me whether or not I'm allowed to join her, so I lie down on my bunk, throw a blanket over my eyes, and listen to the click, click, click, of his pieces against the tiles, only getting up to take more pills or wander to the bathroom whenever I'm feeling particularly nauseous.

"You're taking too many," Finn says when my alarm—turned down the lowest volume to avoid the headache—goes off to let me know that it's time for my fourth Advil of the day.

"I'm taking what it says to on the box."

"You should save it though. If you hold off longer between—"

"I'm fucking sick!" I explode. "Sorry," I catch myself instantly. I need to get better at not fucking up. "Sorry, I'm just... feeling like shit makes me act like shit."

They shrug. "It's fine."

"It's not. This isn't on you. I'm..." I sigh. "I promised to be nicer and I'm seriously trying. These are just exceptionally hard circumstances to be nice under."

"Okay."

I lie down only to sit up a moment later when something hits my bunk. I stare at the box of Advil.

"Finn."

He doesn't look up at me. "You're clearly worse off. You need it more."

I'm supposed to argue because she would, but I feel like shit, so I add it to my stash. "Thanks."

They just nod. "How long have you been sick?"

"I noticed it a day or two after we opened the hatch," I admit. "I'm sorry, I should've—"

He holds up a hand. "Stop reminding me, I was just trying to figure out how long it takes to progress. I can't afford to be mad right now. We need to like each other."

"Okay."

"Is it... bad?"

My brain screams at me any time I dare to move my head a millimeter. I throw up half the food I get down and standing for more than five minutes leaves me exhausted. My entire left leg is now all scabs.

"No," I say. Freaking out can decrease your body's ability to fight sickness and disease. "I've always just been a baby about being sick. It's just like... a cold plus nausea."

"Do you have a rash too?"

"A cold plus nausea plus a rash," I correct. "It's seriously nothing. You feel pretty okay, right?"

"Yeah," they say. "So far."

I really hope that they're not doing the same thing I am.

Rory: Day 19 in the Bunker

"This house supports sex segregation is sports."

I groan, rolling over on my bunk. "Sleeping."

"It's the middle of the afternoon."

I sigh, lifting my pillow off my head to glare at him. "I'm—"

"I know you're sick, but not doing anything will just make it worse."

"Fine." I've been keeping my loonie in my pocket now for easy retrieval, so I pull it out and flip it on my way down the bunk. "Your pick."

"Opp," she says, predictably. "Five minutes to prep?"

"I'll only need two."

Except, in the middle, I stop. "This is my thing," I realize.

"This is an extremely me motion."

"No, I... debate. It's—"

"I literally run the team, Rory."

Team hierarchies shouldn't matter at the end of the world, but it still feels like rubbing salt in the wound.

"I'm not saying that you're not also good at it, it's just not your thing. You weren't going to come to regionals even if we did qualify."

Finn shrugs. "It would've been during tech week. I'd rather let you down than an entire cast and crew. No offense."

"Can we do that?"

"What?"

"I don't know a—" I squeeze my eyes shut, waiting for a particularly strong bout of dizziness to fade away. "Tech week thing?"

"The whole point of those is preparing for when you're performing? With technology? And other people?"

I roll my eyes. "You know what I mean. A performancey thingy?" I consider it. "Preferably not a super loud performancey thingy?"

Finn considers. "I still have my script? With my stuff? We could run it. We'd have to share the script though; I only know my lines."

"Sure. Let's do that."

"It's like, a two-hour production."

"Then it'll kill a lot of time."

She squints at me. "You want to run lines. For a play."

"Yes."

"For two hours."

"Sure."

"Instead of debating?"

"I guess."

They grin. "Holy shit. You like me, Rory."

I feel my ears go hot. "I promised to pretend to. That's not—"

"You like me," she sings.

"We've run a ton of motions. Maybe I'm just getting tired of them."

"You'll never get tired of them."

He's got me there, so I just sigh. "Just get the fucking script before I change my mind."

I'm functional for the whole two hours it takes to get through Finn's script, even if I have to sit down for most of it. After resting for a bit, I'm even able to pretend my way through dinner. I almost make it through the whole day.

And then, I fall down my ladder.

"Rory!" Finn's at my side so quickly that I half wonder if she was there the whole time, just waiting for me to fall. He leans over me, brown curls enveloping his face.

"I'm fine," I shove away their reach hands, pushing myself up onto my elbows.

"You're not."

"I'm fine," I repeat. "It was barely a fall."

"Rory."

"I'm. Fine."

She sighs. "You're using the bottom bunk from now on."

"I don't–"

"You're using the bottom bunk. And I'm grabbing your stuff. No more climbing."

I nod, shifting to the side so they can get around me.

Instead of leaving after setting up my backpack and blanket on the lower bunk though, Finn sits down.

"You're getting worse."

I roll my eyes. "I've been getting worse the whole time. That's pretty much how mysterious illnesses work."

"Rory. I'm... I am too? And if you keep getting worse and I keep getting worse we won't be able to... we need help. And at this rate pretty soon neither of us'll be okay enough to help each other."

"We'll figure it out," I lie. "Not like we have a ton of other options."

They look towards the hatch. The ladder I haven't even stepped near for weeks.

"That's a shit idea," I say before he can even suggest it. "That's probably why we got sick."

"It could've been the food," Finn suggests. "Or the water."

"It's all just dust out there, Finn."

"Maybe that's just right here. Maybe if you'd walked around a bit, we would've realized... everything else might still be fine."

I roll my eyes. "You're being stupid."

"We can't wait until neither one of us is good enough to do anything. If we go look for help–"

"You're the one who didn't want to open the hatch in the first place. It'd be a suicide mission."

"And staying here waiting to die isn't?"

I sigh. "Who goes then, huh? Do you want to?"

She sucks on her lip. “We go together.”

“That’s the least sensical option. Then we’d both die.”

“We’ll flip a coin then.”

“I’m not risking my life because a fucking coin told me to.”

“You did before.”

“I didn’t think anything was actually wrong before!” I sigh, nudging them with my feet so I can lie down. “You’re tired, okay? You’re being impractical.”

“Someone has to go.”

“Then you can.”

I feel them freeze.

“I don’t want you to,” I correct. “It’s stupid. You shouldn’t, okay? We’ll figure it out from here. Let me sleep.”

“Fine.” He gets up. “Goodnight.”

I hear Finn moving a few hours later. I panic. I’m worried he’s done it. I’m worried that she’s convinced herself to go look for help that probably doesn’t even exist.

I squeeze my eyes shut. If one of us deserves to survive the apocalypse, it’s Finn. But if selfish people get to live, then I’m glad that I’m the selfish one.

Rory: Day 19 in the Bunker

I can name every part Finn's ever played in every production he's ever done. I know all of their favourite and least favourite foods, shows, and songs.

It's important to know your enemy.

Rory: Day 20 in the Bunker

Finn is still there when I wake up. There's no dust near the hatch so unless they managed to clean it up while I was asleep, it hasn't been opened.

I'm more relieved than I should be.

She's right. We're both getting sicker and sicker with no sign of recovery. If we want to beat this, one of us will probably have to leave.

It makes the most sense for it to be him.

Finn's the one who's more convinced that there are actually still people out there. Finn's the diplomat. Finn's the one who can stand the longest without falling over and even before we got sick, they were the more athletic one. Finn is the logical potential sacrifice, even before factoring in personal bias. I can't say any of that though, because Finn's the kind of person who would never even consider asking someone to sacrifice themselves for her. It's why he suggested going together. If I suggest that they be the one to leave—no matter how clearly I spell out the logic or how many times I tell her that it's nothing personal—it'll hurt her feelings. I need him to get there himself.

I don't stoop low enough to feign symptoms, I just let myself actually feel them. It's not manipulative to curl into a shaking ball when it feels like my insides are trying to escape my skin. I've been avoiding seeming symptomatic, so it's just me preserving energy when I stop putting effort into that and let myself groan aloud and vomit with the bathroom door open.

Finn doesn't offer to go search for help. Instead, because he's Finn, he tries to take care of me.

It's a day full of "are you okays?" and head towels and checking if I need anything. Constant doting and supervising that would feel suffocating if something about spending almost a month with only Finn for company hasn't tricked me into thinking that they're sweet.

"I'm fine," I say because I'm supposed to. "You're sick too. You don't—"

"You're worse. We're focusing on you right now," she says, because she's Finn.

And I let her.

Finally, at night, he tries again. Finn sits at the edge of my bed, resting a tentative hand on my knee. "We should go," he says. "If we leave together, we might—"

"I can barely make it to the storage room right now, Finn."

I wait. This is where they offer. Finn Williams' biggest chance to prove that everyone else has always been right about him.

She says nothing. Just squeezes my hand, whispers, "get better," and returns to their bunk. And I can't even hate her for it.

Deep down, I guess Finn's just human too.

Rory: Day 22 in the Bunker

I get worse fast. I think maybe the universe is trying to punish me for pretending to give in to my own helplessness because only a couple of days later, I actually have to. I'm a hodge podge of every sickness I've ever had all at once. Too hot and too cold and dizzy sitting, standing, or lying down. Coughing and vomiting almost everything I try to eat back up almost instantly.

I am a waste of supplies. This is not going to end well and in the meantime, I'm eating up double and triple helpings to try and sustain myself. I'm wasting our resources. I'd like to think that if it wasn't obvious that Finn was also slowly getting worse and probably wouldn't need everything, I'd tell her to stop wasting them on me.

I know I wouldn't.

I should have died on impact. We deserved to die on impact. But if I didn't get to do that, I'm going to fight to live until my final breath.

"I've started a journal," Finn collapses at the foot off the my bed when she gets back from the washroom. Probably from vomiting, but she's still okay enough to hide it. "In case I... for when they remember that we're out here and come for us. I bet we'll be super famous."

I smile. "Our parents'll be so proud."

"You should too. For the history books. Or... maybe just for the people who care about us. Just in case."

"That's okay."

"I could write for you. If you just want to dictate."

I sigh. I can't tell them that I'm hoping that all the people I cared about are long gone. Not when he's so determined to hold on to the hope that they're all out their thriving. "I'm tired, Finn."

"I know. Stay up and talk to me anyway?"

I groan.

"I'll just keep talking if you try to sleep. I'll... annoy you into entertaining me."

I laugh. "You're bad at being me."

"They're big shoes to fill." She sits up straighter. "Tell me about you, Rory Wilkens. For the history books."

I roll my eyes. "You already know everything about me."

"History books don't."

I make myself roll over to face him. I will not leave her alone at the end of the world. Not yet.

"I was born in this shit little town so unimportant that the biographer will probably just sub it in for 'four hours outside of Toronto' because that's the only thing outsiders know it as. I was nonbinary. I was pan. I only ever dated one person and I'm not sure if I liked her that way or just liked being able to prove that I was datable because I broke up with her over basically nothing. I cared way too much about debate for someone who'd honestly be pretty mediocre anywhere that wasn't a small town, maybe because my parents were both lawyers and it felt like some stupid way of connecting with them, maybe because I just liked fighting people. Then I got trapped in a bunker for a month. The end."

"Sounds kind of bleak."

"It ends with me trapped in a bunker with the person I'm supposed to hate, Finn. That is bleak. It wasn't... I was never planning on being good at being a teenager. It was just supposed to be a thing I got through so that I could be a kickass adult. Which I guess was all for nothing now so... bleak."

"Just because the world might be a bit different when we get back to it doesn't mean you can't still kick it's ass."

I'm glad I'm too tired for my sigh to be noticeable. "Okay," I play along. "Maybe. Hopefully it'll get less bleak then. What about you? For the history books."

She pauses to think. "I was also born four hours outside of Toronto. To a mum who wasn't single yet but would be. The oldest of four and the only non-girl which was... a lot. Good a lot though. We were all pretty close. I liked acting and dance and pretty much attention of all forms. I'm going to be a performer, it doesn't matter what kind. I'm a lesbian. I've never been on a date with anyone, boy, girl, or otherwise, but that doesn't make me any less of a lesbian."

"Why?" I interrupt.

They frown. "What? Can't comprehend that girls aren't constantly throwing themselves at me?"

"No, I... feel free to tell me to fuck off—I probably would—but why lesbian?"

"I only like girls? That's generally what lesbian means. And like, I guess nonbinary people would be an option too, but I only know one in real life and they're kind of a dick so..."

I roll my eyes. "You're such a bitch."

He's quiet. I think I'll finally get some sleep, but then I realize that she's just paused to cough.

"You're just taking that as answer?"

I shrug. "It was one, right?"

"It wasn't the one you were looking for though."

I'm quiet. It wasn't my place to ask in the first place.

"Does it bug you?" Finn doesn't drop it. "That I use lesbian?"

"It did for like a month or two," I admit. "when you first came out. Only because I was in my weird gatekeep-y 'there's only one way to be queer correctly' phase though."

"Ah, the overly righteous accidentally slightly offensive baby gay phase."

"Exactly. Nonbinary lesbians are a super common thing anyway. I was just being stupid."

"They're not supposed to look like me though."

"Finn, that's—"

"Don't pretend that's not a thing. You only asked because they're not supposed to look like me. We have basically the exact same gender identity but if you wanted to identify as a lesbian, basically no one would bat an eye. It only becomes an issue when it's people like me."

I sigh. "That's not... you know I know you're not a dude. We could talk it in circles a million times and that's not going to change."

"I know. I don't mean to keep making it sound like I'm accusing you of anything I just... I guess I spent forever letting people assume that they knew my labels better than I did? I know you're not doing that, but I never argued about it when I should have and you're kind of the only available person left to argue with right now. Sorry."

I hit her shoulder. "Never apologize for my favourite past time."

They roll their eyes.

"I didn't mean to..." I pause to cough. Finn jolts, ready to help. It's definitely what I was supposed to do when they did the same thing a minute ago. I'm going to get better at that. "I wasn't saying that you shouldn't use lesbian, just that I didn't really get why? Like, if nonbinary people can fit into all labels and you only like girls, it's objectively easier socially to ID as straight, right? So—"

"I'm not queer for attention," he interrupts.

"I know," I say slowly. "Obviously."

She winces. "Sorry. Again."

"Stop apologizing. Again. I guess I just figured nonbinary people who do ID as lesbians normally do it because they're AFAB and used to identify that way or because they figure that that's the dynamic most of society is most likely to see in their relationship. And that AMAB people who use it do it because they're more feminine leaning which you're like, extremely adamant that you're not. I swear I was genuinely just curious."

"I know."

"You don't have to explain yourself. It was fucked of me to ask. I am henceforth blaming all future screw ups on being sick."

They smile a bit. "I actually think you've been a lot more tolerable lately."

"That's not the sickness, it's you being a bad influence."

Finn rolls his eyes. "For me, I guess it's actually kind of the opposite? Like, believe it or not, I'm actually extremely aware that most people see me as a guy still, I just don't know how to fix that. Androgyny's a lot more demanding when you're assigned male. Male's the default so unless you go hyper feminine you're kind of stuck there and I'm not... I don't think that's my thing? Performing gender for other people kind of defeats the whole coming out thing." They flex their fingers. "Nail polish is sick though. Definitely making this a permanent staple when we get back to everyone else. Anyway, to me at least, labels have always mostly been for other people? I'm not a guy or a girl but when people look at me, they always go to guy first so lesbian feels more descriptive. Like, if I liked a straight girl, I wouldn't necessarily not date them, but I'd also be a lot more worried that they'd think I was a guy the whole time. People never jump to girl so I wouldn't have to be all insecure about that in a sapphic relationship so it just feels more comfortable, I think. And when I'm old enough for dating apps I'd stick to the wlw sides because while I'm sure some straight people would take the time to read my profile, figure out that I'm nonbinary, and then swipe accordingly, that'd feel a lot less likely to happen there?"

I roll onto my back. "Ugg, only liking one gender sounds like hell."

"It does get extremely complicated when you don't have one, yeah. Was that... that makes sense though, right? I'm not trying to invade a community or anything, I just—"

"I definitely don't get to decide if that makes sense for you."

"I know, but—"

"Finn. It's the end of the world. Like you said, I'm sure gender norms are practically done being abolished by now. And if they're not," I add "I'll help you throw anyone who tries to police your labels out the airlock myself, okay?"

The threat is made a lot more pathetic when I start coughing so hard immediately afterward that it pulls my body into a seated position.

Finn's hand is feather-light on my back. And warm. So warm. Maybe we're both running fevers.

"I was just fucking with you," she whispers, easing me back down. "about you ruining all nonbinary people for me. I've definitely had crushes on nonbinary strangers and stuff. Just, for the record."

"Good for them," I yawn, curling in on myself. "Did this count as talking, do I get to sleep now?"

"Sure." Finn helps pull up my blankets. He gently squeezes my arm. "Get some rest. Not for too long though. I fully intend to keep bothering you in the morning."

"Can't wait."

The worst part—the mortifying part—is realizing that that isn't a lie. I drift asleep remembering exactly where each of their fingers had been.

Rory: Day 22 in the Bunker

Sometimes—a lot of times—I have felt more defined by Finn Williams than by myself. They were my first interest. My first obsession. My first enemy. My first experience with anger and disappointment and revenge. I spent my entire childhood training to become a master on Finn Williams. She's defined almost every part of me, so I've memorized him in turn. I don't think there's a single person alive who knows more about her than I do.

Of course I would end up liking him. There was never a universe didn't end with me liking him because Finn's the kind of person you can't look at for too long without realizing that they're incredible.

It was supposed to happen years from now though. In university or maybe later. I'd flip through a yearbook, come across their picture, and freeze. It wouldn't be the first time I'd seen her in years. Probably not even the first that month. I would definitely grow up to be the kind of person who cyberstalked him constantly just to make sure that he wasn't doing better than me. But for some reason, that one particular time, something would be different. I'd rub my finger across their face and realize all at once that at some point, I'd definitely had a crush on Finn Williams.

They'd probably be far away, of course. At some other school in some other program. Maybe I'd try to reconnect, maybe I wouldn't, but I would inevitably find out years after high school.

It was not supposed to happen now. It was not supposed to happen when I still have to see her every day.

I remind my brain of this over and over again, but it refuses to think of anyone else.

Rory: Day 23 in the Bunker

"What the fuck, Rory!"

It's not what you want to wake up to the morning after realizing you like someone.

I blink, waiting for my eyes to adjust to the light. I have to push myself against the headboard to sit up because of how close Finn's hovering. I don't realize how red their eyes are until mine finish clearing up.

I grab her arm, instantly awake. "Are you okay? What–"

He hits my shoulder. "You weren't waking up!"

I smile groggily. "Sorry. I'll try to do better next time."

"You're such an asshole!" She pulls away to wipe at her face. "I was trying for fifteen minutes and you wouldn't fucking... you can't do that, okay? You're not allowed to do that again."

I sober. "I'm sorry, okay?" I catch their fingers because if they keep wiping at their face, I'm going to have to acknowledge that he's crying over me and that will destroy me. "I'm fine. Everything's okay. I'm just lazy, remember? I'm fine."

"You're not going to be though!"

"Finn." I squeeze her arm. "How long have we known each other?"

"Since kindergarten," they whisper.

"That's right. Fourteen years. I've been annoying you basically our entire conscious lives. How many apocalypses have we survived together?"

"One."

"Exactly. You don't get to get rid of me this easily, okay? Not over some bullshit illness. I'm sticking around just to spite you."

"Promise me."

It's a stupid promise. An illogical promise. But the end of the world renders all logic moot. "Okay," I say. "Of course. I'm outliving you, remember? That's always been the plan."

He pulls me against his chest. He smells like sweat and vomit because she's also falling apart right now, but I let myself be held anyway because I swear I can feel their pulse through their chest. It feels good to be so physically reminded that other people still exist.

She remembers that we are not the type of people who hug each other the same moment I do and abruptly pulls away. It's hard not to feel cold in his absence.

"I'm sorry," she says, smoothing out my covers. "That wasn't... sorry."

Reason truly no long exists because somehow, I find myself reaching for him. "Finn, that wasn't–"

They stand up. "I'll go take care of breakfast."

"Okay." I pull my arm back. "Thank you."

"Stay awake, okay?" She adds. "No napping today."

"Wasn't planning on it."

When Finn returns, it's not just with water and food, it's with a suspiciously familiar box. I push myself to sit the rest of the way up because there's no way I'm actually seeing things right.

"Finn, no."

She sits down and starts cutting it open. "You're sick, Rory."

"Taking weird conspiracy nut drugs is not going to fix that!"

"Neither is sitting here doing nothing."

I push them away. "The odds of them magically guessing the exact sickness we'd catch and getting the exact type of pill to fix it are pretty much non-existent. At best they're just sugar pills some scammer sold them."

"Or, maybe they were made by someone who spent a lot of time researching the types of reactions that would occur when an asteroid hit."

I roll my eyes. I'd never pegged Finn for an idiot. "I can't believe you're even entertaining this."

"Just take one. Please. It can't possibly hurt."

"It could kill me!"

"I woke up to you dead!" He jumps to his feet. "Do you get that? I woke up and I couldn't even tell if you were fucking breathing! You're dying one way or another, Rory. Take the fucking pill."

When the world's biggest optimist is telling you that you're probably going to die soon, it's hard to takes things lightly. I can't help it. I've been doing so well supressing things and pretending to function, but that's all it takes. I start to cry.

"No." Finn pushes the box aside to sit down beside me. "No, no, no, I'm... I'm sorry. I'm so sorry. I didn't mean to yell, okay? Everything's going to be fine." They wrap an arm around my shoulder and rub my side. "I'm just paranoid. You know that already. I've been paranoid this whole time."

"Don't you dare lie to me about my own life."

"Okay," she whispers. "Okay, I'm sorry. I just... I was trying to help."

"Of course you are," I smile, bumping his shoulder with mine. "You're disgustingly good. That's your whole thing."

"I'll take one too," he says. "If you do. We can both–"

"Finn, that's stupid. There's absolutely no reason we should both be guinea pigs."

"Wouldn't it be less scary though?" She offers. "To do it together?"

I sigh. "Get me some water. I'll take it."

"You're sure?"

"Absolutely not, but if I die suddenly and horribly, at least I'll get to haunt you, right?"

"Rory!"

"Get me water," I say. "Please."

The pill is round, long, and pink. It smells slightly fishy. I hope that's all it actually is.

No matter how many pills I've taken this last week, my brain won't let me swallow it. Brains are tricky like that, always striving towards self-preservation even when that's no longer an option. I have to try five separate times to get it down and by the time I do, my mouth tastes slightly of chalk. I down the rest of the cup just to get rid of the taste.

Finn kneels down in front of me, eyes scanning me over and over again.

I roll my eyes. "I'm not suddenly going to drop dead."

"You're feeling okay?"

"It was in a capsule, Finn. It'll—" I pause to cough. "Those take a while to work."

"Oh," they say. "Right."

"I was lying, for the record," I say, just in case. "I wouldn't... if it does make it worse and I come back as a super cool ghost, no hard feelings. You're right. Not trying wouldn't have ended much better."

They shake their head. "You said you'd haunt me so now you're stuck with that, okay? No leaving me alone here. Even if you die."

"Okay." I swallow. "Deal. I promise to scare the shit out of you at least daily if I die first."

"Ditto."

I yawn.

His eyes go wide. "You said you wouldn't—"

"Calm down." I pat her hand. "I'm staying up until nighttime. Someone's got to keep you sane."

They nod. "Thank you. What do you want to... can you umm, do much?"

I snort. "Probably not. You're gonna have to entertain me." My mouth tugs into a slow grin. "Actually—"

Finn sighs. "I'm going to hate this idea, aren't I?"

"I hear our hosts have quite the extensive literature collection."

"Rory."

"Pleasssse read me sexy alien porn?" I whine.

"I'm not doing that."

"Pleeeeassse."

"I'm not—"

"Imagine I die in like an hour and you refused to honour my final wish." It's a dirty move. Also one that they should have seen coming.

"Holy shit, Rory!"

I grin. I've won.

I'm pretty sure Finn grumbles to himself the entire way to the storage room.

"How are you feeling?" Finn checks for the billionth time once it's finally late enough for me to justify going to sleep without freaking her out.

"Perfectly normal levels of shitty."

They sigh. "I want to move our mattresses to the floor. Or at least mine. So I can get to you quicker if it abruptly activates and you end up choking on your own vomit."

I grin. "That your way of asking to sleep with me?" The only way I know how to cope with realizing that I like Finn Williams is joking about it so overtly that he hopefully won't catch on.

"Rory, you're dying. I probably am too. Just slightly slower."

"That a yes?"

"Rory."

I sigh. "Fine. You have my permission to sleep together. The boring way. On different mattresses."

"Thank you." They're weak too, so it's clearly a struggle to get both mattresses onto the floor, but considering I broke a sweat just moving off of mine, I'm in no position to help. `

I lie down facing the ceiling, stiff as a board. Finn's technically a whole mattress away and at this point has seen me cry, scream, and vomit more than anyone else has ever been allowed to, but it's lying down on the same floor that feels too intimate.

It is exceptionally inconvenient to develop crushes in the middle of end times.

I close my eyes and do my best to pretend that she's not there and just when I think I've almost done it, she speaks.

"Rory?"

"It's late. Let—"

"Do you hate me?"

I flip over so quickly that I'm convinced my brain's forcefully extracted itself from my skull and remains behind on the pillow.

"What?"

"It's okay if you do," he fiddles with the top of his blanket. "I'm just... I really don't want you to? Which I know is selfish, but—"

"Finn. You're the good one, remember? I'm the one who's insufferable. I have literally no reason to hate you."

"I made you open the hatch," they whisper. "I made you open it and now we're dying and—"

"I would have died anyway if we hadn't."

He shakes his head. 'We could've had years, Rory. We could've had years and I fucked it all up."

I frown, shifting closer. "I would have opened it that first day if you hadn't stopped me, remember? You bought us more time, not less."

"We should've opened it together. That would've been fair. We—"

"That would've been stupid. I never would have stood for it." I keep my eyes on hers and find his hand with mine. "I've known you pretty much as long as I've known how to know things. I—we're—I mean, fuck Finn. I've known that we were supposed to hate each other longer than I've known my own fucking name. I can't... you're disgustingly good and apparently freakishly sincere about all of that and I get that and appreciate that but I can't... I'm going to keep being a dick. I need to keep being a dick because fighting with you has always been the most constant thing in my life and now the rest of my life might not even exist anymore, so I need to pretend that just that one thing hasn't changed, okay? I know that's not fair and I'm trying to balance it with what you need too but I can't stop... that's not your fault though. You haven't done anything wrong. I pulled you to the end of the world with me and you've actually been freakishly nice about it. None of this is on you, okay?"

"I... you what?"

I sigh. "You didn't even want to come. But you did because you're a good person and you'd do anything to make other people happy and I knew that and I used it against you. You shouldn't be here right now. I'm..." my voice catches. "I'm so, so sorry."

"Rory," they say slowly. "I'm pretty sure my family isn't actually safe and happy in some government tunnel system somewhere."

"I know, but—"

"If you tricked me into anything, it was living."

"For what! To spend a few weeks trapped with me knowing you're going to die?"

He shrugs. "It wasn't an awful few weeks, right? Not entirely? I wouldn't... I wouldn't go back and stay." This, I believe, is true.

"I wouldn't go back and not open that hatch." This, I know, is false. "So it's no one's fault, okay? It's that fucking asteroid's. And the government's for not telling us about that fucking asteroid."

Finn raises our clasped hands into the air. "Fuck the government!" They exclaim.

I laugh. "Fuck asteroids!"

"Fuck all the governments!"

"Fuck the entire universe!"

I yawn, nuzzling my head into my pillow. We let our arms fall, but don't disconnect them.

"Finn?"

"Yeah?"

There are a million things to say. I am incredibly aware that this might be my last chance to say anything at all. "I..." I yawn. Let my eyes fall closed. "Fuck you, Finn Williams."

She laughs. "Fuck you too, Rory Wilkens. Have a good sleep."

Rory: Day 24 in the Bunker

I wake up.

I wake up and Finn's alarm isn't even going yet. I wake up and sit and don't immediately feel like falling back over. I wake up and walk to the bathroom and brush my teeth for the first time in days. I wash my face and brush my hair and go to the kitchen and make oatmeal that actually stays in my stomach.

I'm pretty sure the sketchy apocalypse pills said one per day, but I don't let myself check.

I like Finn Williams. I've come to terms with the fact that I really care about Finn Williams. That changes absolutely nothing. I've never wanted her to die, but I would have taken all the medication if it came down to me or her. I can't let myself near the box until he's awake.

"I'm going to kill you," they announce when they finally wake up and join me in the kitchen.

I grin. "Good morning to you too. I made breakfast," I slide her a bowl across the table.

"Rory! I woke up and you were gone! I was worried something had happened!"

"That I'd what, died and sunk immediately down to hell? Got kidnapped by the invisible man?"

"I–" Finn's face goes red.

I grin wider.

"You suck."

"Thank you."

He sits down across from me. "You're feeling better then?"

I nod. "I mean, definitely still far from perfect, but a lot less die-y than yesterday. Pretty sure your weird pills worked."

She frowns. "Rory, I don't know if we should–"

"Nope," I point my spoon at them. "Too late. You accidentally saved my life, now you're stuck with me forever."

He sighs. "It could be placebo."

"Don't ruin it, yeah? If it is a placebo, let it keep placeboing."

"Okay," Finn nods. "Fair enough."

"Maybe wait a day or two before you take one? Unless you suddenly get way worse. Just in case." I swallow a glob of porridge. "Can you actually go grab them? I want to check and see when I'm good to take one again."

Her brow furrows. "You're sure you're good?"

"Yeah. Loads better, seriously."

"So much better that you still can't go grab the box yourself?"

I choke on a glob of oats. "Just... you should grab it, okay? We should divvy it up and... I shouldn't be the one who grabs it."

He nods, finally catching on.

Then, comes the hard part.

"I don't think we should do fifty-fifty," I announce.

Finn frowns. "What?"

"I'm a lot worse than you, right? And had more direct exposure. There's not a ton of them so I think it's smarter... you feel fine, right? Or functional? We should do sixty-seven thirty-three."

He frowns. "If you need more and I have more left I'd obviously give them to you."

"I know!" I do. It's what makes it awful that I'm bargaining. "I'm just... I would too. I swear, I really, really, hope I would too, but I'm worried that if I get too in my head about not having enough I might try to take them?"

Finn blinks. "You're telling me that you'd steal them. That's what this is. I give you more or you steal them."

"I don't want to!" I try to explain. "I'm... this is all so stressful, Finn. I just... it's the perfect opportunity to fuck up and I really don't want to fuck up. If I feel more confident in how many I have, I won't."

She just stares.

"Plus it's fair, right? I was way worse. Even if it's only because you got sick later, we're catching it earlier for you. I'd probably need more anyway."

They're still quiet.

"Finn. I'm sorry, okay? I know I suck. I'm just... I don't think I'm backing down on this."

She sighs. "Flip for it."

"What?"

"I'm not backing down either. We flip for it. You win we do it by thirds, I win we do it by halves."

"Okay." I say. "Fine." I pull out the coin. We watch it spin. I let it land on the table so he'll know that I haven't interfered.

Tails. Shit.

"That's that then." Finn starts splitting it up.

"If you needed half, I would have given you half. You know that, right?"

She sighs. "I'm seriously not mad, Rory."

"You can be though. I–"

"We were both fully convinced that you might not wake up this morning. You're allowed to be a bit paranoid."

"You're too nice," I point out.

"I know," they nod. "It's why we work. Most people wouldn't be able to put up with you."

I cup a hand over my mouth, prepping for a wave of nausea in case I have to run to the sink.

Finn's frowning when I remove it. "You're sure you're doing better?"

"It's not like it'd go away in a day. I'm getting better though. I can tell. Stop worrying, okay?"

He looks skeptical, but nods.

Rory: Around Day 27ish in the Bunker

I hear an animal somewhere. Clawing and running and making this weird chirping sound. It's probably just in the walls. I don't know how it could have possibly gotten in here.

I bet it's still going to cause problems though. I'm too distracted to pay a lot of attention to it right now but I bet later, it'll cause problems.

Rory: Day 28 in the Bunker

I do get better. It happens quickly. After a few days of taking the pills, I feel almost all the way back to normal—minus a slightly raw throat.

Finn does not.

I can't tell why. They started taking the pills on day three and seemed a lot more functional the next morning, but then they started getting worse again almost immediately.

Whatever's in the pills can make people better. Just not Finn.

I have been trying to rid myself of Finn Williams for over a decade. I'll be damned if I let some mystery sickness do it first.

She smiles when I return to the main room with lunch. He's a shivering, sweaty mess, but he still smiles because of course he does.

"You want jerky and crackers or slightly chewier jerky and crackers?"

"Mmm. Normal chewiness please."

I fix their pillows before handing them a plate.

"Look at you taking care of me."

I roll my eyes. "I'm shit at this. I'm no good at gentle. That's why you have to hurry up and get better, okay?" I rub her shoulder. "Gotta set the universe back in order."

"I'm sure it'll kick in soon," he whispers, even as his eyes flutter shut.

"Eh!" I hop up onto their bed, kicking her shin. "No falling asleep. If you made me live by your schedule for that long, you don't get to get out of it just because you're not feeling good. Debating, talking, board game, or alien porn?"

He rolls his eyes. "They have normal books too, you know."

"Finn, the objective here's staying awake."

She looks down at her lap then holds up a hand. "They're all chipped and gross now." I don't point out that their nails are definitely one of the most decent looking things about them. "I want to... fix it?"

I nod. It feels good to have a task to do. "I can do that."

I pull over my bag, find the red nail polish, and kneel down beside their bed to get to work.

"I think I've figured out your secret," he whispers.

I freeze, mind racing to figure out what she's talking about.

"You're nice."

I roll my eyes, glancing up at them. "Shut up."

"You are though. And you secretly care about other people. It's all very embarrassing."

"I do not. I'm just bored enough to be helpful right now."

"Have you ever had a panic attack?" He abruptly changes the topic.

I move the brush slightly further away, just in case. "Why? Are you feeling—"

"I'm fine. Just curious."

"No," I say, grateful for the subject switch. "I don't think so."

"Your parents?"

"If they did, they'd never admit to it," I wince. "Not that... it's a super common thing. There's literally nothing wrong with that."

"Alice? Anyone else you secret admit to caring about that I don't know about?"

I sigh. "Just because I don't know anyone else who gets them doesn't mean it's like, a character flaw or something. You have enough of those already, I don't need to invent new ones."

"When did you learn what to do during one?"

"What?"

"You didn't know in elementary school. When did you learn?"

I roll my eyes. "That has nothing to do with you. I just like to be prepared for every situation. I didn't like that I wasn't."

"Nope. You cared about me. You've secretly wanted to be friends forever."

"We're not even friends now, stupid. We're... reluctant allies."

"We've spent almost a month looking out for each other."

"Yes. As allies do."

Finn sighs. "You're so fucking stubborn."

I look up to make sure that she's smiling before continuing with their nails.

"You're a pretty decent one though," I admit. It's the closest I can get to 'I like you'. It might be the closest I'll ever get. "as far as allies go."

Finn laughs. It rattles with phlegm. "Thanks. You're absolute shit."

Rory: Day 29 in the Bunker

Finn starts coughing so loudly in the middle of the night that it wakes me. I jump out of bed and to their side to help them sit up.

I'm terrified that they'll choke.

"Sorry," they croak when the fit lets up for a few seconds.

"Shut up."

"I woke you."

"Shut up."

He keeps coughing. It feels like hours, but he keeps coughing. I don't know what I'm supposed to do. I get her water, but it doesn't help. I find a lollipop at the bottom of my bag, but she just spits it back out a few seconds later and keeps coughing. I'm too scared that doubling up other medications with the pink pills could be dangerous, so I do the only thing I can. I sit. I wait. I help hold onto their shoulders when the coughing gets so bad that I'm genuinely worried they'll whack their head against their own lap. I pull sticky bangs off of her face and rub her back.

"You can get back to sleep," he wastes the next time he gets enough of a reprieve to talk on saying. "If you want."

"Shut up."

I don't know how long it takes for it to stop. Maybe it never does. Maybe she just passes out. I wake up the next morning with half my body still on their bed, Finn's head heavy against my shoulder. I check her pulse before easing out from underneath her and fixing their blankets. His alarm's ringing, somewhere. For once, they've slept through it. I find her phone in the sheets, turn it off, fix his hair, and go to make breakfast anywhere where I can pretend that Finn Williams isn't dying.

Rory: Day 30 in the Bunker

"If I ask you to write in my journal, promise not to look at any of the pages before it?"

It's a cruel thing to ask. If it were anyone but her, I'd consider it calculated. Finn has to know that I would have said yes to anything he asked for days now, no matter how much I've been wondering about what they're writing.

"I thought the whole point was to get it published. Global renown."

"Maybe I wrote some not so flattering things about you that I'd rather not have you read while we're trapped in close confines."

I snort. "Fair. Permission to go through your bag and steal your diary?"

"Promise you won't read it first."

"Fine. Promise."

He nods. "Permission granted. Just like... flip really fast over the other stuff."

I make myself. It is incredibly hard to make myself.

"Okay," I get the pen ready. "What am I writing?"

"A note to my mum."

I freeze. "Finn. I'm not sure..."

"I'd do it myself if I wasn't pretty sure my handwriting would be illegible at this point. Nothing mushy or sentimental, I promise. I know you'd kill me for that."

"Okay." We're back to pretending that she's out there, then. "What am I writing?"

"Dear mum. I love you, I miss you, hug the girls super, super, tight for me, okay?"

"Was the okay for me or her?" I clarify.

"Her."

I add it. "Got it."

He waves a hand at me. "Let me sign it."

I hand it over. Finn's handwriting has always been neat. It used to infuriate me in middle school. Now, even though they're only writing four basic letters—and one of them a repeat—it's illegible.

She hands it back. "Add P.S. I'm nonbinary. I've been using she, he, and they for years now and I'd appreciate it if that's what you wrote on any obituaries or tombstones."

I almost drop the pen. "Finn."

"Write it. Write it and finish getting better and go fucking tell her one day, okay?"

I swallow. There's no way to say no. "Okay."

I close the journal and slip it back into their bag. "Your mum then? That's who you're not out to?"

She nods. "And my little sisters. They're not like... transphobic," he quickly adds. "Or at least, I don't think they would be? I don't know if you've noticed but I kind of have a people pleasing issue and I guess... I didn't want to give them the opportunity to be let down by me."

"They'd be letting you down. Not the other way around."

"I know," they say. "Principle wise, I know. It's just... fuck! It seemed so much easier to just not tell them because I figured I could later? And I guess... they wouldn't and I know they wouldn't but I was terrified that they wouldn't love me the same way anymore? But now all that leave me with is never knowing for sure if anyone could see all of me and still love that. I thought I was making things easier, but now I'm probably going to fucking die before anyone—"

"I love you."

I'm not sure what reaction I'm expecting, but it definitely isn't a violent fit of laughter.

I cross my arms and wait for them to finish. "Asshole."

"No! No, I'm sorry." The fact that they're still giggling makes that difficult to believe.

"I'm an incredibly non-vulnerable person. You could've just emotionally scarred me forever."

"Noooo," she whines, making grabbing motions at me. "Roryyyy. I'm sorry."

I roll my eyes, sitting back down beside them. "Asshole."

"I wasn't trying to guilt trip you into saying you loved me. That was just... extremely out of left field."

"I do though, for real. And I've been watching you go through pretty much every disgusting bodily function imaginable these last few days, so I'm pretty sure that checks the having seen all of you box."

He blinks. "Rory. That's... very sweet in a very you way, I guess. But you're not in love with me."

In no possible universe did I see myself ever having to convince Finn Williams that I have a crush on her. "I've known I had a crush on you for weeks now," I admit. "I probably actually did have a crush for longer."

"Well yeah, same, but that's because we've spent a month trapped together in a high stress situation. That's not enough time to fall in love."

"When is?"

"Well," they pull my hand under the blanket with theirs. "For starters, I'm pretty sure you have to wait longer than the first time you're even willing to tell someone you like them."

"Woah, no one said anything about liking you. This is all still deeply upsetting for me."

She laughs. "See? I'm pretty sure that also means that we're definitely not there yet."

"Then we'll both just have to stay alive long enough to get there. It'd be pretty pathetic, dying before it happens."

"Deal." He lets his head fall onto my shoulder. "I can't believe you admitted it first."

"Shut up."

"Like, I'd obviously noticed how completely and utterly obsessed with me you've become, but I figured I'd have to confess at least three times first then threaten you before—"

"Shut up! You were being all sad and pathetic and I was just trying to fix it. I just don't know how to do the good person thing in moderation yet."

They grin. "You want to be a better person for me."

"If I tried to suffocate you with your pillow right now, I bet you wouldn't even be strong enough to fight back."

She sinks down against me, letting her eyes fall shut. "It would've been fun, I think. Falling in love with you. Tedious and definitely maddening at times, but fun."

"It will be," I whisper. "I'm pretty great."

"Okay. Sure."

Rory: Around Day 30ish in the Bunker

"Also, you need to stay long enough to fight whatever's in the walls if it escapes. I'm not good with animals."

"What?"

"The animal. In the walls. I think it might become a problem soon."

Finn laughs. "Okay, Rory. Sure."

Rory: Day 31 in the Bunker

"You're not getting better."

"I might."

"You're not!"

Finn sighs, running a hand through her hair. "I don't know what you want from me here, Rory."

"I want you to fucking get better."

"I don't think that's happening without medical intervention. Which we don't have access to, so..."

I freeze. I know what he's doing. I tried to do the same thing. Yet for some reason, this time, it works.

"Fine, I'll leave, okay? But if it looks hopeless and I don't find anything within five hours of here, I'm coming back."

They try to sit up. "I'll come with you."

"Finn. That's stupid."

"We can help each other out, if we go together."

"You'll be deadweight." It's not an insult, it's just a fact.

"What if you die alone out there?" He whispers.

"Then at least I'll know I tried."

"What if... you can't let me die alone in here, okay? We... wait and see if I get better these next few days first. Please."

"Finn."

"Please."

I wait.

Rory: Around Day 31ish in the Bunker

I wake up to the sound of scurrying feet. The animal or whatever it is in the walls seems desperate to get out.

I know the feeling.

Rory: Day 32 in the Bunker

I am going to kill Finn Williams. Finn Williams has been secretly trying to kill Finn Williams so I am going to kill Finn Williams to avenge her.

I shake him awake. Definitely not as gently as I should, but if they're not taking care of themself, I don't see why I have to.

They wake up groggy and confused. "What—"

"Why the fuck do you have so many pills left?"

Her eyes widen. He goes completely still. "You went through my stuff."

"I wasn't taking anything! I only let myself because I realized I wouldn't even fucking dream of taking anything because I'm way more terrified of you getting worse now than me getting sick again! So why the fuck did I just go to get your pill set up from an almost full bottle!"

They sigh. "Rory."

"Don't do that! They work. We know that they work. Why wouldn't—"

"I have taken a couple. I just wanted to save them. Space them out in case either of us got really bad."

"You've been really bad for days!"

"Rory, I—"

"No!" I am screaming. I'm screaming and crying and if I wasn't half convinced that it would make her cave in on herself, I'd be hitting. "You don't get to put me through that! You're taking one right now with me watching and then one first thing tomorrow while I'm watching and then one every fucking day after that, okay? You're taking them until we both run out because I clearly can't trust you to be fucking honest about when you need them."

"Okay," she whispers.

"You let me think it wasn't working. You let me think I was going to have to watch you die just to save a few pills!"

He sighs. “I was fine, Rory.”

“I wasn’t.”

“Okay,” they grab my hand, tugging down as if that’ll also lower my hysteria. “I’ll start taking them properly, okay? One every day.”

“Thank you.” I pull their body to my body. Forehead to forehead, chest to chest. Then, I remember that I’m supposed to be pissed and shove them away. “You’d better.”

Rory: Day 33 in the Bunker

"You're sure you took one this morning?"

I'm pacing. Finn's been freakishly still for days now, so I'm pacing to compensate.

"Yes, Rory. You basically forced it down my throat."

"That doesn't make sense though. You're—"

"Rory."

"still getting worse. You should be—"

"Rory."

"getting better by now. I don't know why—"

"Sit down? Please?" They pat their bed or at least, they try to. It's more like their hand falls then bounces there. "You're making me dizzy."

I do. I take her hand in both of mine.

"Hey," he smiles.

"If we double up—"

"That's probably dangerous, Rore. It says it all over the bottle."

"So is doing nothing, right? That's what you said to me. You might just not have enough in your system yet."

He sighs. "I might just have waited too long."

"No." I squeeze their hand. "No doing that. You're the optimistic one, remember? I don't know how to be the optimistic one. Take two, okay? Please? One right when you wake up, one before going to sleep."

"Okay," she relents, eyes half closed. They never seem to stay open for that long anymore. "Whatever you want."

Rory: Day 34 in the Bunker

"It's not your fault, Rory."

Finn wanted the light out tonight. She says they're too bright. They probably had been for a while and he just didn't mention it because he knew that I wanted them on.

If they were willing to ask me to turn them off even though they knew I didn't want to, we're fucked.

"What? I know."

I'm pressed against her in the dark because her bunk's definitely not big enough for the two of us. We considered moving the mattresses to the floor again, but Finn can't sit up at all without using the headboard for support anymore. I can hear his breath and I'm sure he can hear mine, but I still keep our fingers locked and wrists pressed together. Pulse to pulse, just in case. Just so I always know.

"You didn't know I wasn't taking them. It's not your fault."

"I know that."

"Rory?"

"Yeah?"

"I can feel you crying."

I know that too.

"You can sleep in your bunk," they whisper. "It's... you're better. You might get sick again if–"

"I'll just take the pills again. Like any sane person would."

"You can still go."

"Do you want me to?"

"I–"

"Nope. Forgot you're annoying. Rephrasing. Do you, Finn Williams, want me to go or stay? You. I'm not asking what you think I want to hear so don't you dare use that as an excuse to lie to me."

"I'm... you can stay. If you want."

"I want."

"I'm not going to die, Rory. We're both just being dramatic."

"I know." I lie.

What I do know is that she's terrified of dying alone and I'm terrified of letting them die terrified. So, I squeeze his fingers a little harder. Pull her pulse a little closer.

I am going to be here for every beat. No matter what.

Rory: Around Day 35ish in the Bunker

I don't think the animal or whatever it is is actually in the walls. It feels too close. I don't know how it got in or how long it's been here, but it's definitely in here with us. It will definitely become a problem soon.

Rory: Day 35 in the Bunker

"Sit with me. Come hang out."

"In a minute." I don't bother trying to wash the sheet Finn vomited up dinner into. I'll have to eventually but for now, we have replacements and I'm needed here. "That was basically everything you ate. I'm gonna grab you something else before–"

"Rory, nothing's stayed down all day."

"It could. You're on Gravol now. Maybe–"

"I'm tired of trying, okay? Sit? Please? I wanna just hang out."

I sigh, giving in. I leave the sheets in the bathroom and return to their bed. Finn's the one who suggested sitting together, but we both know that he won't be able to. She shifts closer to the wall to give me space after I've propped up her pillow a bit.

"You know," he says slowly. Everything they do is slow now. "I always thought you'd be shit at taking care of people. I thought I'd be doomed."

"Shut up," I whisper.

"But you're not. Because we've always done this, haven't we? We've been taking care of each other for years now."

"Maybe you have. I hated you until a few days ago."

Finn laughs. It's wet and sticky and frankly disgusting, but it's a laugh so I take it. "You're so full of shit."

"Maybe," I admit. I slouch down to meet his level and drop my voice to a whisper "but you'll never prove it."

Her arm–long, lanky, and lazy--finds my shoulder. "Fuck you."

I grin. "You too." I hesitate. Watch them breathe. "I'm sorry though, for the record. If I ever... not for not liking you, but if I ever didn't like you a bit too much."

"You didn't. At your best you were like, mildly annoying."

"I think I definitely got better than mild a few times."

Finn shrugs. "Guess I never really paid that much attention to you."

"Asshole."

"Not really though. I thought... I guess I thought we'd be friends? After I came out? Not that all queer people are, obviously, but—"

"Yeah," I swallow. "I know. I knew. I'm sorry."

"But apparently that just pissed you off more so—"

"It didn't," I stop him. "I mean, not you. It... I think you were able to move on after middle school because you're the better person? Not in the like, 'bigger, more forgiving way' but probably that too honestly, just... debate's been my whole thing since I was nine and you just showed up on a whim and crushed it. Who does that?"

She doesn't respond. I bolt up. "Finn?"

A warm hand tugs my arm back down. "Still here. Just figured you'd keep complimenting me if I stayed quiet."

I roll my eyes. "I'm a secret hypocrite, you know. It was a lot easier to blame most people not liking me on them being bigots than acknowledging that I'm kind of a mess and then you had to come out and ruin all that because everyone's fucking obsessed with you. I think I decided that that meant I had to overanalyze every tiny thing we did differently as a reason they'd like you and not me instead of acknowledging the glaringly obvious shit personality one?"

"I don't think your personality's shit," he says. "I mean... not entirely."

I snort. "Like, I used to get so pissed on absolutely no one's behalf that you didn't show up to everything wearing fucking pride flags because I'd decided that that was cheating somehow but even if it was... I hate makeup. It bugs my skin and makes me feel more like a doll than a person and it's just... uncomfortable. And I still wore it every single tournament because I'm a fucking hypocrite and it's sometimes exhausting needing to remind the world that you're yourself over and over again? You genuinely use he/him and I somehow decided that that was you betraying your identity even though I'd be standing right next to you wearing something that actually did feel like betraying mine because I knew it would make me more palatable to judges."

"It never suited you, by the way."

I laugh. "Gee, thanks for letting me know four years too late." I sigh, sinking back into the pillow. "I've always been exactly myself and that turns people away and you were there being you and everyone was eating it up so I decided that it had to be fake. It's not though, is it? You're just nice. It's disgusting."

"I've never... I like those parts of you, I think. The exactly yourself bits. Maybe I could do without some of the several layers of fake bitterness you hide it all under, but I've thought you were pretty cool since I was old enough to."

I roll my eyes. "Bullshit. I was an asshole."

"It's not bullshit," he shrugs. "But it might've been. I do that a lot, for other people. You don't. That's kind of badass. I've always wanted to be more like that."

"We could merge together and almost be a functional human being."

"You never know, you've been willingly talking about your feelings for a whole few minutes now. I think I'm making you functional already."

"What about you?"

"After this? After this I'm not wasting time on anyone else's bullshit."

I roll over to face her. "I would like to propose an alliance," I declare. "When I inevitably take over and become president, you can be my VP. I'll handle all the shady backstabby stuff, you'll be our public image person. That part's always seemed exhausting."

"You want to be president?" Finn checks.

"Yes."

"Of Canada?"

"It's an apocalypse, Finn. Anything can happen. President sounds more universally impressive than Prime Minister."

"Okay," she nods. "I'm—"

She doubles over into a new fit off coughs. I jump up to get them more water.

"Sorry," he whispers when he's done.

"Only you would apologize for coughing while sick."

"We were having fun. I ruined it."

"You didn't ruin anything."

I refill the cup in case we'll need it again and climb back onto their bed. "That time seemed a lot calmer than normal, right? I think you're getting better."

He sighs. "Rory."

"You could be."

"I'm definitely not. That's fine though, I'm ready."

"I'm not," I whisper.

"You will be," she smiles. "Thanks for buying me an extra month. It's been fun."

"No one's dying."

"Rory. You need to be ready."

"Shut up. You don't get to tell me what to do."

They just sigh.

"You're the one who has to make it, okay? That's what makes sense. You're... I'm not a bad person. I like to think that I'm slightly above average, actually. But you're fucking great. It's not allowed to be you."

He coughs a bit more, apparently not done. "I've been lying to you, Rore."

"What?"

"I almost... I did lock the door. After... you were right. For a second, I panicked and I locked it."

"That's okay," I squeeze her fingers. "That's... I would have done the exact same thing. You opened it again. That's what matters."

"It wasn't even because I realized that it was awful of me though. I just... I decided that it would be worse to be alone. I opened it for me."

"That's okay," I repeat. "I would've done the exact same thing."

"I tricked you though! I acted upset that you'd even thought I could have because I needed you to think that I was a good person then I got pissed at you for basically the same thing and... I wasted two days! I wasted two whole days just because I wanted to trick you into thinking that I was better than I am!"

"Finn." I slip my free hand under their chin and gently angle it towards me. "You're the best person I've ever known."

"I'm not though," she shakes tears onto her pillow. "I'm—"

"I like you when you're being all nice. Yeah, sure, it's admirable or whatever. I'm sure other people appreciate that too. But my favourite you is always going to be loud and angry and maybe a little bit mean. It's why I like annoying you so much. I'm selfish and obsessed with getting you to prove that you're actually human."

"This isn't a healthy reaction to someone telling you that they were going to let you starve to death, Rory."

I roll my eyes. "Shut up, you were never going to be able to follow through with that." I tuck my chin into his shoulder. "I wouldn't have been able to either, for the record."

"I know."

"You're the only thing that makes the end of the world even remotely bearable. I would've caved after a day tops."

"I know. Me too."

He might kiss the top of my head. He might just let his head fall their then cough a little. I'm too comfortable to check.

"I know it took a literal apocalypse for us to become friends," she says. "But I'm glad it finally happened."

"We're not friends," I correct on impulse.

"You can't keep doing that. You already fucked up and said you loved me."

"That's different. Purely infatuation. I actually still can't stand you."

"Yeah?" he whispers.

"Yeah," I whisper back.

She smiles. She sighs too, but it's light and free so I focus on the smiling part as her eyes fall shut. "You're such an asshole."

"Thank you," the words stick in my throat.

"Good night, Rory."

I start to roll over, but their grip on me goes tight. "Just getting the light."

"Stay," they say. "Leave it on."

"Sure. I'll see you in the morning."

"Sure."

Rory: Day 36 in the Bunker

I open my eyes and Finn's not beside me. I jump up so quickly that I hit my head on the top bunk.

She can barely move on her own. She shouldn't be moving around on her own. But if they're not here, they clearly did and they clearly didn't wake me up first because they're Finn fucking Williams so of course they didn't. Which means that they've passed out on the floor somewhere.

The ground's bare though. The bathroom's empty. And then, from the kitchen, whistling.

I throw open the door and they're restocking the cupboards. "Oh, hey," she says. "You slept in."

I run at him. I should worry about knocking him over but I'm still shaking off panic, so I run. I throw my arms around their chest and hit their back a few times for good measure before letting go.

"You asshole!"

They grin. "Doesn't feel great to wake up to a terminally sick person missing, huh?"

"Asshole!" I swing at her again.

She catches my fist. She's strong enough to catch my fist.

"Hey," he says. "Morning."

"I'm... you're feeling okay? It's working now?"

"Looks like it."

"That's... how? Why?"

They shrug. "Maybe it was doubling it up? I don't know, it worked pretty suddenly for you too and I'm trying not to over think it. Thank god for weird conspiracy drugs."

"You're okay?"

"Still feel like I was run over by a truck once or twice, but at least now it doesn't also feel like I was buried alive immediately afterwards."

"You should've woken me."

He shrugs. “That’d kind of negate the whole valuing my life thing. I took a bunch of stuff out of storage, by the way. I think I trapped the animal in there so we should probably avoid it unless we absolutely need something.”

I blink. “I... what?”

“The animal? The one we’ve been hearing for a while now? That’s why we’ll have to avoid the storage room for a bit.”

I’m too shocked from seeing them standing again to focus on anything else. I don’t know how they’re managing. “Oh, right. Smart.”

I knew it would become a problem eventually.

“I found extra pills too!” She shakes a little capsule of them. “They must’ve fallen out of the box before we got it. Now we’re extra prepared if something goes wrong again.”

“Amazing.”

Finn frowns, cupping the side of my face. “You’re crying, Rore.”

I laugh. I’m delirious.

He smiles. “Wow, you’re really happy I’m okay, huh?”

“I’ll kill you if you tell anyone.”

“I’d expect nothing less.”

She pulls her hand away. That’s when I catch it. The nail polish on their thumb’s started chipping already.

“I’m painting your nails again,” I decide.

“What? They’re basically fine. You did it a few days ago.”

“I’m painting them.” I don’t know how to articulate that I have to. That I won’t be able to fully believe that he’s okay again until they’re perfect.

“I can do my–”

“Let me,” I stop him. “Please.”

“Sure.” She shrugs. “Knock yourself out.”

I work slower than I ever have before. I make them perfect because I’m okay and he’s okay and everything else is too. I keep her fingers in mine as I work instead of on the ground and I swear I can feel her heartbeat in each and every joint.

Rory: Day 37 in the Bunker

Now that Finn doesn't need me anymore and I can climb again, I try to sleep on my top bunk. But whatever we've trapped in storage—Finn says she's not even sure, all she saw was a flash of fur—must not like its now smaller captivity, because even though it's on the other side of the bunker, its running keeps me up all night.

"Finn," I whisper, giving up on tossing and turning.

"It keeping you up too?"

I nod. Somehow, even though he's below me and not facing me, he knows that I do.

They sit up, pull their knees up against them, and pat the other side of their bed. "Come hang out."

I hurry down the ladder.

We don't though. Somehow, she ends up lying back down and then I end up lying back down and then we're falling asleep.

I have never been a fan of change. That was why I'd thought that returning to the bed that I'd spent the most time in would help me fall asleep more easily. But maybe at some point this last week, I've decided that Finn's bunk is where I belong.

Rory: Day 38 in the Bunker

Finn doesn't say a word when I go straight for their bunk the next night.

Hopefully that means that they've decided the same thing.

Rory: Day 40 in the Bunker

Finn gets better just as quickly as I did. In a matter of days, they're back to bouncing and pacing and setting way too many alarms.

Something horrible has happened to me. I actually find it endearing.

We play board games and do puzzles. We debate and read scripts and books. I watch them exercise.

But it's almost like without an ongoing disaster to focus on, we remember. We're stuck. We're bored. And we don't know what's coming next.

Rory: Day 42 in the Bunker

"I think we need to get serious about leaving, Rory."

It's a heavy thing to suggest over crackers and peanut butter.

"What? We're fine. This is basically the first time we've had no reason to leave."

"We might get sick again."

"We won't."

"We'll run out of food eventually."

"Not for a while."

She glances towards the storage room. The running stopped a few days ago. Whatever was in here with us must have been living off of our opened food because once we trapped it with only sealed stuff, it died. Or went super quiet. We haven't risked opening the door to find out yet and we'd have nowhere to dispose it anyway. If it's decaying, we can't risk getting trapped with the smell and any potential diseases.

I sigh. "We still have tons. And everything's sealed anyway. One of us can just run in there and plug their nose or something. We'll flip for it."

"We can't stay here forever, Rore. There could be people out there."

"What if there's not? What if we would have been fine here then we open that hatch, get sick again, and end up dying for nothing?"

"Would that be much better than dying alone down here?"

I frown. "You said you weren't upset that we survived. You said you were glad."

"I was, but—"

"We're enough, me and you. We're enough. We're not risking that."

She sighs. "Fine. Whatever."

Rory: Day 45 in the Bunker

Finn's a genius. He memorizes the entirety of their play. She eagerly pulls me into the main room, sits me down on my bottom bunk, and forces me to watch all two hours of them performing as every single part.

They would have been good at this. They should have gotten the chance to be good at this.

Finn deserved to be adored by the masses but if the only person left to witness them is me, I'm never taking my eyes off of them.

Rory: Day 47 in the Bunker

"We should set a date," Finn suggests in the middle of Monopoly. "And once we hit it, one of us leaves."

"I'm not leaving, Finn."

"There could be people out there."

"Then they can come find us!"

"What if they don't know where we are?"

I sigh. I don't want to push it. I'm terrified she'll declare that if I don't go, she will. Of course, she doesn't.

Finn would never leave me alone in the dark.

Rory: Day 49 in the Bunker

I kiss them. It's our first one so I make sure to do it right after we've both finished brushing our teeth for the morning. First kisses have to be perfect, so ours tastes like the archetype of good breath.

She laughs. "What was that for?"

"Just to celebrate. Us. Beating an apocalypse."

He laughs again then kisses me back. He rubs at my cheek. I think it's a caress but then they say, "crying again, Rory."

I roll my eyes. "Tell anyone I get sappy and overwhelmed and I'll deny ever knowing you. Now," I hand them a glass of water. "Take the pill."

Finn rolls their eyes. "I've practically been fine longer than I was sick at this point, Rore."

"I don't care. I said I'd make you take them. Take it."

She does.

Rory: Day 50 in the Bunker

"One of us needs to go, Rory."

"No."

"We need to go."

"Shut the fuck up!"

I throw a book at them.

"Sorry," I pull myself into a ball. "Sorry, I didn't mean... I'm sorry."

"I'm fine. See?" She spins in a circle to show me. "I'm fine."

I sigh. "Let's not talk about it, okay?"

"Okay."

"I'm sorry."

Rory: Day 52 in the Bunker

We're cuddling on his bed when I finally make myself say it.

"You know I've been fucking with you, right? We're friends. I know that. I'm... I'm sorry I couldn't... we're friends."

She laughs against my hair. "Yeah, Rory, I know. You're nowhere near as covert as you think you are. I've known the whole time."

Rory: Day 53 in the Bunker

"We need to–"

"Stop it."

Rory: Day 55 in the Bunker

"What if one of us just–"

I lock myself in the kitchen.

Rory: Day 60 in the Bunker

"Fine."

I plop down on her bed.

"What?"

"Fine. We can go. You're right, we can't just stay here forever, especially with our supplies cut."

"Thank you," Finn says.

"Shut up."

She kisses my hand. "I'm proud of you."

I look away. "I'm not five."

"Do you have your coin?" He checks. "We'll flip for it."

"I... what?"

They sigh. "I really like you Rory, but I'm not about to offer to go off into a potentially deadly wasteland for you. Pretty sure you're not going to either."

"You want to go together," I remind them. "That's your whole thing."

He sighs again. "That's the least logical decision we could possibly make here, Rore. This is serious. We have to think this through."

I jump off their bunk. "You're not doing this right. You're supposed to be the one who suggests we go together."

"Rory..."

"You're fucking getting it wrong! I'm supposed to get to be the logical one!"

She pinches her brow. "We can't go together, Rory. That makes no sense. It has to be you."

"Or you, if you lose the coin toss."

They nod. "Or me if I lose the coin toss."

I consider it. "No. Not yet. We still have time."

"Okay. Whatever."

Rory: Day 61 in the Bunker

"I bet we'd be famous, you know. Once one of us goes out there? That'd be fun. I've always wanted to be famous."

"Shut up, Finn."

"Okay. I'm sorry."

Finn: Day 24 in the Bunker

"Flip for it."

Rory looks confused but then, Rory looks confused by a lot of the things I say. Rory also looks alive.

"What?"

"I'm not backing down either," I tell them. "We flip for it. You win we do it by thirds, I win we do it by halves."

"Okay," they say. "Fine." It's the only sign that they're not actually as okay as they're pretending to be. Nothing's ever this easy with Rory. But they're also standing and breathing and finding something stupid to argue over. They're fine. Or at least, they're getting there.

They start to throw the loonie then catch it mid-air.

"I've changed my mind, actually." I know that they don't mean about taking most of the pills. They're Rory. It's how they work. I also know that they have a lower opinion of themself than anyone else left alive, so it doesn't matter. Rory will give me extra pills if a third ends up not being enough for the same reason that they won't let themself handle them on their own. They just refuse to admit to giving a shit about anyone else, even if they'd only be admitting it to themself.

I still haven't decided if that's more adorable or infuriating about them yet.

"Are you okay with being heads? Hasn't exactly been working for me recently."

"Sure," I shrug. It doesn't matter. If the pills are really why they suddenly seem so much better and there aren't enough, we'll either both die or both live. We'll either get better before hitting the third point or work our way back to fifty-fifty.

They throw, it spins, it lands on tails.

"That's that then," I start splitting it up.

Rory grabs my arm. "Finn. I didn't... you don't have to worry, okay? I'm just being paranoid. If you need more—"

"I know. I'm seriously not mad."

They sigh. "You're too nice."

I've mastered not wincing at things like that. If you do, people might start to realize that they're wrong about you. "I know. It's why we work. Most people wouldn't be able to put up with you."

They roll their eyes, we load the pills into our bags, and then it's done.

Rory: Day 63 in the Bunker

"What if we debate it?" Finn suggests.

"What?"

"Whether or not we leave. Let's debate it."

I roll my eyes. "Okay, one: we stay here, we live."

"Point of information!" he declares.

I roll my eyes again and wait.

"Would you not agree that you going is the only shot we have at actually feeling alive?"

I pull my pillow over my head. "Stop doing that. Stop trying to sacrifice me."

"Rory, I–"

"You're not doing this right!"

She sighs. "We'll try again tomorrow."

Finn: Day 26 in the Bunker

It's not a placebo.

Rory's random surge of energy wasn't their body getting ready to finish giving up. Instead, they get better so quickly that it seems impossible. They start keeping down meals again and their cheeks fill back out. Their eyes lose their glossy sheen. They go back to nitpicking and eye rolling and argument starting and for a moment, it almost feels worth it. Like if the universe had to end to let me see Rory come back to life again, I'd hit self destruct each and every time.

Rory: Day 64 in the Bunker

"Isn't it weird that we haven't even bothered coming up with a species for it yet?"

"What?"

"The animal?"

"Shut up, Finn."

Finn: Day 27 in the Bunker

I take the first of my pink pills because they'll notice if I don't, but I have a plan. I don't need them yet. I'm still doing better than Rory was when they took their first one. Rory won their two thirds, and if they need them, they're keeping them. I can deal with being a bit sick. I'll take one as needed when I actually need it, just in case something else goes wrong.

Rory: Day 65 in the Bunker

"It's probably near when graduation would be," I say. "Or prom."

I have no idea how accurate that is. If I counted out the days, it would probably be horribly wrong. But I need something to distract us that's not fucking leaving.

Finn's great. They're wonderful. Except for their insistence on bringing that up. I'm choosing to believe that that part of her doesn't exist.

"You think so?"

"I bet you would've been valedictorian," I admit. "I was so ready to be pissed about that. I'd already let Alice know the specific type of ice cream she'd have to buy me to cheer me up when it happened."

"What was it?"

"Cotton candy."

"Excellent choice."

Finn pops off their bunk and slowly walks over to me. "Go to prom with me, Rore?" He says. I knew he was going to. It's why I brought it up.

I roll my eyes. "Extremely lame as far as promposals go. I thought you'd do better."

"I had limited material to work with," she shrugs. "Plus, I knew I wouldn't have to worry about you saying no."

"Shut up."

They hold me against their chest and we sway back and forth for hours. I close my eyes and trust him to guide me. As long as my eyes stay closed, everything is going to be alright.

Finn: Day 29 in the Bunker

It's terrifying, not being in control of your own body. I've been sick before, but the kind of sick that you can hold in to keep from scaring the people around you. But when my body wants to cough, it does so endlessly and relentlessly. When it wants to vomit, I can rarely make it all the way to the sink.

I'm exhausted. I'm beyond exhausted, I'm some lesser form of existence that comes when you push too hard against it. But I cough until I'm certain that my lungs themselves will come flying out if I do it even once more then force myself to stay awake until I'm sure Rory's asleep. I can't take a second pill without them thinking that I'm doubling up.

And then, I see it. Their bag just sitting there, half open. No matter how many times they urge me to keep mine away from them, they've never done the same. Rory's always overestimated me a lot less than other people tend to, but that doesn't mean that they're immune to it.

I'm not sure why I do it. I already have more pills in my bag than I should. I swallow one of theirs down with water then slip five more into the side pocket of my bag, just in case I run out. They still have more. They still have enough.

And, I know exactly where to take more from if I need them.

Rory: Day 66 in the Bunker

"If you're so deadest on staying here, you should at least turn off the lights at night to save power," Finn says.

"It's supposed to last months."

"If you're not ready to go now, are you going to be then?"

"Stop it. I don't like the dark. You know that. You're just being a dick."

She squeezes my hand. "I'll be right here with you though, right? So there's nothing to worry about."

My breath sticks. "The lights stay on."

Finn: Day 30 in the Bunker

I've been waiting over half a decade for Rory Wilkens to admit that they have a crush on me.

It's just not supposed to be a misguided deathbed confession.

"I love you," they say.

I want to take it. For once in my life, I want to grab on to something I know I don't actually deserve and refuse to let go.

I've been waiting over half a decade for Rory Wilkens to admit that they have a crush on me, so I can wait a bit longer for them to love me and actually mean it.

So, I laugh.

And they get offended and faux-mean and completely back to being themself which means I've made the right decision.

People have told me that they liked me before. Nobody's ever accidentally jumped to love, but in hindsight, it's the only way I could ever see Rory doing it. They wear their feelings all at once or not at all. It's just how they work.

People have told me that they liked me before, but it's never been the actual me, so I've never said it back. It wouldn't be fair to let them keep thinking that they liked me when they'd actually just fallen for the version of myself that I'd carefully curated to be the most appealing to them.

Rory's hated some part of every version of me. They've always had this infuriating ability to see through the bullshit. So, it's Rory then, who tells me not when I'm flirting or acting or mirroring. Of course they do it when I'm weak enough to not even bother perfecting something as basic as my own signature.

Rory: Day 67 in the Bunker

"What's the point of living if no one sees you doing it? Didn't someone say something like that? Some philosopher or something?"

I sigh. "See? This is why I'm supposed to have that side of the argument. You trying to do it makes no sense."

"Leaving alone's the only thing that makes sense, Rore."

"Not yet."

"You can do it. You know you will eventually. This way at least you still have pills left over."

"Not yet."

"Soon though?"

I don't respond. I don't want to let him down.

Finn: Day 31 in the Bunker

Rory's noticing. Of course they are, it wasn't like them making a hasty recovery and me basically not making one at all would be subtle. I was ready for that.

But then they threaten to leave.

I'd start taking the pills daily, just to stop them. I've never been as selfless as I pretend to be. I'd eat up all of our resources if I thought it'd keep them from leaving me alone.

But the one I took two days ago didn't do anything. I'm too scared to find out if the next one won't either.

Rory: Day 68 in the Bunker

"Good morning!" I kiss Finn's nose then shove a glass of water in her face before he can respond. "Take your pill."

They roll their eyes. "This is stupid, Rory. You're wasting them."

"Making sure we keep you here isn't a waste. We promised to stay long enough to fall in love. We haven't finished doing that yet."

He pulls me into a hug. Kisses my hair. Then, against it, whispers, "soon though."

Finn: Day 32 in the Bunker

My head's spinning when I wake up. "What–"

"Why the fuck do you have so many pills left?"

I freeze. They know. "You went through my stuff," I say. I know it's not the right response, but I'm not used to seeing Rory genuinely angry. They think that I'm accusing them of the very thing I that I actually did and I don't stop and correct them. They're screaming and crying and angrier than I've ever seen them, but I don't correct them because even though they've seen me at my physical worst–maybe because they have–I don't want them to know the truth.

I promise to take them. I don't tell them that I have reason to believe that that might not do anything at this point.

Rory: Day 69 in the Bunker

"You're crying again, Rory."

I throw something. Anything. Everything. "I told you to stop fucking pointing it out!"

Finn: Day 33 in the Bunker

Rory keeps leaving their bag alone around me. I slip the stolen pills back in while they're in the kitchen.

Rory: Day 70 in the Bunker

"What if you start by just going a few hours out and then—"

"I'm not leaving without you," I cut Finn off. "Just stop it, okay? I'm not going to agree to that. Neither of us are going by themselves."

They toss another peanut butter cracker into their mouth and sigh. "Going together makes no sense. Be reasonable here, you need—"

"I don't give a shit!" I exclaim. "Together or not at all."

Finn: Day 34 in the Bunker

I'm not used to Rory not bothering to hide their emotions. Maybe they think that I'm less perceptive now that I'm this far gone, but I can still see them pacing and muttering to themself. I even catch them crying when they're not fully aware that I'm looking.

I should tell them that I took the pills. I should tell them that I've had access to theirs this entire time and would have spaced mine out whether or not I'd had more to begin with. It wouldn't be fair for me to let them think that this is at all their fault just because I decided to be an idiot. They have to wake up twice that night just to save me from choking on my own saliva and we both know that that's not going to work for much longer.

So, under cover of dark, I say, "It's not your fault, Rory."

"What? I know," they lie.

"You didn't know I wasn't taking them. It's not your fault."

"I know that."

"Rory?"

"Yeah?"

They're crying. Their shoulder is pressed so firmly against mine that I can feel them crying. I choke down my confession. I'm sick and broken and probably dying and they're solid. Warm. Somewhere, I know that they won't hate me for telling them. Somewhere, I know that they're not actually only lying here with me because they're blaming themself for this.

I'm not used to trusting that people will stick around if I let them see too much truth.

I know that they won't hate me for telling them, but they might want to be angry, just for the night. They might climb up to their bunk and ignore me until the morning.

It'd just be a few hours, but I don't have a lot of those left. I change the topic. I ask them to stay. And I know, somewhere, that they're not only doing it because they feel guilty, but I'm not ready to let go of that safety net yet.

Rory: Day 70 in the Bunker

Finn sighs, getting up to hug me. "Oh Rory. We both know that's never going to work."

Finn: Day 35 in the Bunker

I wake up and know.

I've always thought that that was a myth. Something old people said on their death beds to convince their loved ones that they were prepared and wouldn't necessitate mourning. But I wake up and it's nothing I can pinpoint---I'm worse, but not significantly worse that I've been waking up any other day—but I know.

Sometimes it's just time to go.

I decide that I'm not going to tell them, though I think Rory catches on too. I never fully understood why they seemed to feel guilty that we hadn't died at the moment of impact, but now I do. It's not fun, waiting for it to come. I want to live until the very last moment.

I'm going to tell them about the pills. I get them to sit with me and promise myself that I'm going to tell them because this is my last shot. I get them to sit down with me but then I can't figure out how to turn the conversation there and then they try to get up—for nothing, just the light—and I remember how terrified I am of them not being there when I go, so instead I say, "stay."

They do.

"I'll see you in the morning."

I wonder if they also know that I'm probably not lasting that long.

Rory: Day 70 in the Bunker

I hit her. I hit and punch and bite and scratch. "It was supposed to!"

"I know," he says.

"We were supposed to do everything together!"

"I know. I'm sorry."

"I was supposed to have years left to pretend to hate you! We were supposed to fucking fall in love."

"Rory." They catch my fists. "Enough. It's time to go."

I shake my head. I breathe in snot. "Not alone. You can't make me do this alone."

"Okay," she slides her hand down my arm, squeezing my fingers. "You win, okay? Together. We go together."

I smile. "I've always been better at debate."

He laughs. "Fuck you, Rory."

They guide me to the storage room then stop. "Close your eyes, okay?"

"What?"

They sigh. Their face wavers. "I can't be in two places at the same time, Rore. Just—"

My eyes are already closed. My nose is plugged too. I wait a moment to make sure it's safe, take his hand, and enter. I hold my breath and squeeze my eyes shut until we've left the room, but I know I won't be able to forever.

We walk towards the ladder.

Finn: Day 36 in the Bunker

I try to sleep.

I tell myself that that's all it is. Close my eyes and go to sleep. Easy.

I can't do.

There are a million things that I was supposed to say. A million things that I was supposed to do. But it's coming. It will soon. I have to choose the last couple of things I want to accomplish before it's too late.

"Rory," I shake their arm in the early hours of the morning. I don't know if I'm doing it weakly because I've lost most of my grip strength or if I already know that I don't actually want them to wake up. "Rory!"

I give up too quickly. Maybe I wasn't trying in the first place. I could wake them and say goodbye properly. I could come clean and leave nothing unfinished. They wouldn't be mad. Not now. It'd probably help them, in the long run.

But they'd be sad. I've spent too long being happy for everybody else to let my final moments be sad.

So, I watch them breath. I lift my aching neck and kiss their forehead. I put my fingers in theirs, my head on their shoulder, and press my ear against their pulse to listen to their heart beat.

It does. Slow and steady and calm and beautiful. I listen. I don't wake them. I let it carry me away.

Let the records show that in their final moments, Finn Williams chose to be selfish.

Rory: Day 70 in the Bunker

I hesitate at the top, but I haven't forgotten anything. I have food, water, pills, and a journal. Bandages.

And them. Always them.

I hold her against my chest, shifting the bulk of the sheets to one arm. It's more secured now. Wrapped tight enough that I don't have to worry about keeping my eyes closed.

"Ready?" I check.

"Ready." From below and above and everywhere. From right behind me. I choose to believe that it really comes from right behind me. I grip the sheets tighter. I take a breath. With the other I reach up to the sky, turn the handle, and push.

Acknowledgement & About the Author

Thanks as always to all of my early readers for the help with this one. Specifically Brie Cannon, Anjuga Raveendran, Ryn E., L. Brennan, Gryffin Langston, Alaina Kelley, El H., Meadow Bush, and Zeynep Y. who all somehow managed to get me feedback back within my insanely small window.

Alex (any pronouns, feel free to talk about me behind my back at will I'm impossible to mispronoun) published their first book after turning 20, promptly decided to publish a book a month those next ten months because that was reasonable, and is now trying to hit 22 before turning 22 because he has no concept of time. To join her reading list and get 1 email a month with info on new and upcoming releases, early reader opportunities, genre polls, and other polls (Alex really likes polls), message them at alexnonymouswrites@gmail.com

See you next month :)

CWS: swearing (lots of it), lots of talk/potential depictions of death & illness, referenced mispronouncing & deadnaming (no actual deadnaming), the end of the world, vomit

Printed in Great Britain
by Amazon